THAT DREAM
COMES TRUE?

TEKKERS

SETH BURKETT

POLARIS
PUBLISHING

This edition first published in 2020 by

POLARIS PUBLISHING LTD
c/o Aberdein Considine
2nd Floor, Elder House
Multrees Walk
Edinburgh
EH1 3DX

Distributed by
Birlinn Limited

www.polarispublishing.com

ISBN: 9780957507692
eBook ISBN: 9781913538002

British Library Cataloguing-in-Publication Data
A catalogue record for this book is available on request from the British Library.

Designed and typeset by Polaris Publishing, Edinburgh
Printed in Great Britain by Clays, Elcograf S.p.A.

1

'Top bins again. Watch this.' Chloe swept her blonde hair from her eyes, checked her target, took two steps to the left and then curled the ball towards the goal. Its battered panels arced through the air, crashing against the playground wall in exactly the correct spot: the top right corner of the marked goal. Marcus, rooted to the spot in his scuffed black school shoes, never stood a chance of saving it.

'Sick!' Chris cried.

'Mad!' yelled Marcus.

'Absolute tekkers!' Josh added.

Zak watched his best mate with a mixture of pride and envy as she nonchalantly went to retrieve the ball from where it had landed. It should have been the keeper's responsibility to get the ball. It was only fair, seeing as they'd been scored past. But Chloe was never one for wasting time when she could be practising. Now she jogged her way toward the ball, her long limbs seamlessly weaving in and out of the other pupils as they moved in all forms of chaos around the playground. A few yards away a teacher blew sharply into her whistle. Mrs Turnbull. 'No fighting!' she roared in the direction of one particularly savage pile-on. Zak afforded himself a smile. If the pupils at Redwood Community College weren't playing football at lunchtime then they were testing the limits of the teachers. 'He grabbed me tie, miss!' a year 11 called Tom protested as Mrs Turnbull broke up the mass of bodies.

'You see that?' Zak asked Chloe as she returned to the marker they were using to practise their free-kicks.

'I was just about to get involved!' Chris complained. His friends all turned to look at him quizzically. Even Marcus, outraged by what he'd heard, had taken a step away from his goal. Chris wasn't only the youngest in their school year – still months away from turning 13 – but also the smallest.

'Maybe if it was the last thing you ever wanted to do,' Josh replied. 'If you jumped into those year 11s you'd be flattened. Even Zak's twice as big as you and he's tiny!'

'I was going to!'

'Okay, okay, all right children.' Chloe spoke with authority. It was often left to her to defuse situations. Yes, they all agreed she was the sensible one. The hardest working. The one with the immaculate uniform and the perfect ponytail. And, according to at least half of their school year, the best footballer in the whole of Redwood. 'What you got, Zak?'

'Yeah, go on Zak. You always say you're better than Chloe. Now prove it.' Josh liked to egg on situations. At times, Zak felt as if their mate delighted in disputes. But this wasn't the time for a dispute. This was another chance to prove that he was an

2

even better footballer than Chloe. The latest in an epic series of battles that had seen them grow from best mates in nursery to partners in crime on the playground, in the classroom, on the pitch for Redwood Rovers FC.

'Ha, that was nothing,' Zak replied. He liked to play up the rivalry. It was healthy, driving them both on to become better – Redwood's own version of Cristiano Ronaldo and Lionel Messi. 'Pass us the ball, Chloe.'

Chloe smiled as she handed him the battered ball. Every single lunchtime it had been booted around the playground – except on the rare occasions it had been confiscated by Mrs Turnbull for a rogue shot into a gaggle of year 7s or been stolen by a group of bored year 11s. Fortunately such occasions were few and far between. Zak and Chloe's little group were respected in the playground. By and large, they were allowed to get on with their football games. Panels were peeling off and the Panther Sports branding had long since faded. Hadn't it looked so shiny on that first day at Redwood Community College! Now there remained just a faint outline of the Panther logo, drawn just above the valve. Zak placed that valve just above the tarmac. To get the best dip on his shot, that was exactly where he needed to strike it. Like Chloe before, he took two steps to his left. He readjusted the black headband that separated his brown curls from his boyish face. He could feel his heart rate spiking. He'd done this thousands of times, yet each time he found the process exhilarating. Nothing motivated Zak more than proving he was the best.

Than being the best.

Marcus was slightly right of centre in the goal, weight

forward so he could spring into action. The hard tarmac floor didn't usually bother him. There were holes in the knees of both legs of his trousers, marks of previous attempts to save Zak and Chloe's free-kicks.

'Oi!' Chris yelled at a group of year 7s wandering into the goalmouth. 'Get out of the way or else!'

'I bet they're really scared of you,' Josh said, rolling his eyes.

'Did the job, didn't it?' Chris retorted as the year 7s turned back from where they came and were swallowed up by one of the school's long corridors.

Zak shut everything out. There was only one thing that mattered. Not the specks of rain that had begun to fall from the moody sky. Not the wandering year 7s. Nor Mrs Turnbull's new whistles as Tom, the year 11, ran around in delight, twirling his friend's tie above his head. No, all that mattered was him and the battered old ball. He looked at it, checking once more where the valve was, where the goal was, where Marcus was. And then he let loose.

The right laces of his black trainers connected with the ball right on the valve. The ball flew into the air. It looked too high, as if it was going not just over the goal, but over the playground wall and into old Mr Tulip's rhododendron bush. The amount of times they'd had to jump the playground wall to get their ball back from that bush! It was rumoured that Mr Tulip had once locked a pupil in his shed for two days when he caught them in his rhododendron bush. Not that anybody at Redwood Community College could actually remember it happening. But now, now the valve was working its magic. The ball dipped dramatically. Marcus, having shuffled to his left in preparation, now became more desperate in his movements. He dived but it was too late. The ball had already crashed off the playground wall in the exact place it had been aimed at: top bins.

'Sick!' Chris cried.

'Absolute tekkers!' Josh added.

'Argh, my knees!' Marcus yelled as he landed with a crash onto the grey tarmac that now had small specks of red dripping onto it. The hole on the left knee of his trousers was now a gaping hole, a red graze where his knee had made devastating contact with the surface.

'There's no separating them!' Josh responded, ignoring Marcus's cries.

'Marcus, get the ball for us. Zak, Chloe, what else you got?' Chris asked.

'Fat chance of that, I think my knee is falling off!'

Chris sighed. Marcus had a tendency to be dramatic. 'Fine, I'll get it myself then,' he moaned. 'Oi! Excuse me! Pass that ball, will you?' Chris had caught the attention of a small boy by the school gates, his backpack twice as big as his upper body. The boy picked the ball up and threw it to Chris. 'Well, that's my best trick,' Chris admitted. 'Josh, you got anything?'

'A few things,' Josh said with a knowing smile. 'But best to leave it to the experts, eh? So go on then Zak and Chloe, what you got? And hurry up, the bell is about to go.'

Zak took hold of the ball and gave Chloe a knowing look. There was definitely one area where he had an advantage over her. He dropped the ball at his size 6 feet and just as quickly flicked it back up by stamping on it with his heel. The ball rotated backwards, floating up toward his green school blazer. 'Yeahhh!' Chris cheered as Zak then caught the ball on his chest in one swift movement. He held the pose for a few seconds, the ball perfectly still, and then flicked it forward so it was now back onto his right foot. Right foot, left foot, right foot, left foot. Zak's keepy-ups were one flowing motion, his slight legs never in danger of letting the ball drop to the floor. He could feel the eyes on him in the playground. Not just Chloe, Chris, Josh and Marcus, but also other pupils and teachers. He could sense that they were impressed. Time to impress them even more. One around the world. Zak kicked the ball up with his right foot and then circled it with his entire right leg before then kicking it again with his right foot. Two around the worlds. His leg circled around again, drawing its own orbit through the air. Three around the worlds. Now he was into his groove. After the tenth around the world he caught the ball in his hands and locked eyes with Chloe. 'Your turn,' he winked.

'Ohhh!' Chris and Josh yelled in excitement, attempting to egg Chloe on.

'My knee is in so much pain,' Marcus complained, but nobody heard him. All eyes were on Chloe.

'Party tricks are for seals,' Chloe responded dryly. 'You can't score a goal with an around the world.'

Across the playground the bell sounded, signalling the end of the lunch break. Zak and Chloe bumped their fists together as a mark of respect, just as they always did after competing against each other.

'Saved by the bell!' Josh commented.

'Yeah, whatever.' Chloe dismissed him with a smile.

'See you lot after school, yeah?' Zak asked.

''Course,' Chloe responded. 'You don't think I'm going to let you finish on that, do you?'

It was Zak's turn to store the ball in his locker. He took it into his grasp and then walked toward his form room, hastily redoing his tie so as not to ignite Mrs Turnbull's anger. The specks of rain were falling more heavily now. Zak removed his headband, knowing he wouldn't be allowed in the school building with it. There was a uniform policy for a reason, he'd been told many times.

'Yo, that was epic.' Chris caught up with Zak as he steered his way into the corridor. 'Like, serious. That was even better than Baller B!'

'Who's Baller B?' Zak asked. Chris stopped in his tracks, his eyes wide in surprise.

'You don't know Baller B?'

'Nah, who are they?'

'Serious?'

'Serious.'

'Mate, you need to check him out. The guy is sick. He does videos on YouTube. Mainly he does freestyle football videos but the stuff he does is nowhere near the same level as what you do. And he gets millions of people watching his videos. The guy makes millions of pounds from it!'

Zak knew that people made money from videos on YouTube. He watched videos on YouTube himself. That's where he learnt many of his skills. From compilations of Redwood's own Abou Trabt, his favourite player who'd honed his skill in the streets of Redwood before signing professional forms with High Grove

FC, to footage of icons like Ronaldinho and Diego Maradona. He trawled through tutorial videos, breaking complex skills down and copying them until he got them right. But the internet was a big place.

'Like the F2 Freestylers?' Zak asked.

'Yeah but newer, younger. The F2 have been around for ages. Baller B has been big for about a year now.'

'How does he make so much money then?' Zak was impressed and sceptical in equal measure. Chris liked to exaggerate. If he said millions, he probably meant thousands. Which, to be fair, was still a whole load of money.

'YouTube pay you when people watch your video. So do advertisers. Fans donate to their favourite YouTubers. Then when they get big enough, the YouTubers bring our their own merch. Baller B has got his own clothing line.'

'And you honestly reckon I could do it?' Zak's interest was growing.

'Mate,' Chris said in his most serious voice. 'It's not like me to exaggerate.'

Zak couldn't concentrate in double science at the best of times. The science block was the last remaining part of the original school. While the rest of Redwood's buildings had been bulldozed and updated in line with the most modern of comprehensives, the science department evoked the memories of a long gone age. The classrooms smelt of history. Large, single-glazed windows provided welcome distraction as Mrs Sprockett stood at the front of the class and droned on about atoms and electrons. *Millions* of pounds. The thought bounced around his mind. Zak knew that he had talent. What was the worst that could happen? He'd film a video and put it up on YouTube and nobody would watch it. It would hardly be devastating.

'Oxden!' Zak was shaken from his thoughts by Mrs Sprockett's piercing voice.

'Yes, miss?'

'Are you paying attention?'

'Yes, miss.'

'Then you'll be able to tell me about electrovalent bonds?'

Busted.

Zak retrained his view from the window to the wooden desk in front of him. A faint smell of gas lingered in the air. His classmates liked to turn on the Bunsen burners to annoy Mrs Sprockett when she wasn't looking. How he could do with a distraction right now. He stared at the names carved into the desk, names from years and years ago. His own father's name was even carved into one of the tables in class 3A.

Adam, class of '82

Claire rocks, IDST

Keith <3s Patricia

They all stared back at him. Memories of all those in the past who had been unable to concentrate in double science.

'Oxden, if you were listening you'd be aware that an electrovalent bond is one made when an electron from one atom is transferred to another atom.'

'Oh yeah, that sounds right, miss,' Zak smiled. It had the intended effect. Mrs Sprockett's anger lessened. Zak's classmates often observed that he was given special treatment because he was the school football team's captain. They had a point.

'Don't zone out again, that's a warning. Next time your name will be on the board.'

Zak nodded in agreement and spent the final hour of the class doing his best to give the impression that he was paying attention. Something about covalent bonds. Something about currents. Copying out of a textbook. And then finally, finally, the bell blared out and it was time to pack up.

Chloe was waiting for Zak as always. They fist-bumped and then unchained their bikes from the shed.

'I can't wait until I no longer have to do double science,' Zak complained. 'Honestly, it's so boring.'

'You could learn a lot from science, you know,' Chloe retorted. 'There's a lot of science that helps you to get better at football. Different training methods, sport science, recovery.'

'Yeah, but not electrovalent bonds,' Zak pointed out.

'Probably not.'

It wasn't a long bike ride home. The main difficulty was leaving the school. With over 1,000 pupils, the bike shed became a free for all. Pupils climbed over each other to get to their bikes first and leave as quickly as possible. Inevitably, the year 11s were first out. 'Careful!' Mrs Turnbull screamed in vain. 'You're representing the school. Kirsty, are those trainers?'

Once out of sight of Mrs Turnbull, Zak put his headband back on. His black trainers, disguised as school shoes, remained unspotted. Chloe took the lead, pedalling quickly. Everything had a purpose when it came to getting better at football – even cycling home. The traffic thinned out as the pair left the bulk of the school traffic and rolled along the high street, past the hodge podge of betting shops and charity shops, acknowledging the pockets of workers dotting the cafes and pubs with their bacon sandwiches and their English breakfast teas. As the tired shopfronts turned to red brick houses the pair signalled right, emerging onto Upper Street. The road rose gradually, a steady climb that gave a panoramic view over their modest town. It wasn't much, but it was theirs. The red brick houses where their friends and families lived, the mini roundabouts that frustrated even the calmest of drivers, their school, standing proud as one of the few signs of modern times. From here, Zak could see the Redwood Rec, home of Redwood Rovers FC and site of so many of his and Chloe's victories over the years. On the horizon, the abandoned car manufacturing plant, its empty tarmac spaces sprawling over the green moors, eating away at the town: a constant reminder of the devastation that had come when the factory owners shut the plant down and moved their operations to Eastern Europe, where the labour was cheaper. The town had never quite recovered. The workers sought different jobs, Zak's dad included. From building work to call centres to gardening, they spread across different industries, all of the time missing the friendship and sense of community that came with clocking in at the plant.

'Later then.' Chloe's voice, slightly out of breath from the effort of the climb, snapped Zak from his thoughts. They'd reached Glenn Close, the turn in to Chloe's tree-lined cul-de-sac. The nice part of town, made up of a collection of large new-build houses sitting on plenty of private land.

'Yeah, sure. Give me an hour or so,' Zak shouted back.

First, he had a scouting mission.

As soon he walked through the front door of his terraced house on King's Lane, he sat at the kitchen table and fired up his laptop. It was an old laptop and while he waited for it to load he poured himself a glass of water and grabbed a handful of custard cream biscuits. It had been a long day at school and he deserved a treat. Still, the laptop loaded. That was the problem with old laptops. Distracted, Zak looked to see if any of the letters on the chipped kitchen table were addressed to him. Bill. Unpaid bill. Rent statement. Nothing. All boring letters to his dad. Finally, the screen blinked back at him, a collection of icons with a background image of Abou Trabt in action. Zak clicked on the Internet Explorer icon, then moved the mouse to the search bar and typed in 'Baller B.' 3,193,000 results came up on Google. At the top were three videos, followed by Baller B's official YouTube channel and his Wikipedia page. Zak couldn't help but notice that Baller B's date of birth was just two years before his own.

He clicked onto the first video that came up. An advert filled the screen. Zak sighed with frustration. He really needed to install an ad blocker. It wasn't even a skippable advert. He watched on the screen as a dentist told him why Perfect Whites was the perfect solution for healthy teeth. Finally it faded to black and Baller B's video started.

A lanky figure brimming with energy filled the screen. Straight away, Zak could see that his positivity was infectious. 'Welcome, yo!' Baller B yelped into the camera, his hands playing out every word. Dressed in a black hoodie with the hood up and a snapback with the hashtag #BALLR_B that covered his messy blond hair, Baller B wasn't just the height of energy – he also looked pretty cool. 'Today we're going to be taking some goalshots!' Every word was almost shouted. Boom! An explosion filled the screen as the video transitioned from Baller B covering to the screen to him taking his goalshots. 'We've got Z2K in net' Baller B observed as the camera zoomed to the goalkeeper, also wearing a #BALLR_B snapback. Another YouTuber, Zak presumed. 'Now, watch this,' Baller B urged as he struck the ball toward the goal. Z2K dived over the shot as it rolled along the ground. 'Oh!' Baller B screamed in celebration, running first to the keeper and then to the camera in celebration. 'Ballers only!' he whispered. His catchphrase, as far as Zak could make out. The video played out more 'goalshots', more 'Ballers only!' As Zak watched he could tell that Chris was right. Baller B's skills were fairly basic. A garden gnome would have saved plenty of his shots, rather than Z2K who specialised in jumping over the ball. With goalshots done, Baller B moved on to his skills. They were good, but nothing that Zak couldn't do. Baller B caught the ball on his neck, did an around the world and caught it on each foot a few times. 'Ballers only,' Z2K whispered into the camera. Zak could see the appeal of Baller B's videos. They were fun. They were skilful. The more he watched, the more he was convinced that Chris hadn't been exaggerating. And then he searched for Baller B's earnings and he really did find out that Chris hadn't been exaggerating. Baller B really did make millions of pounds a year. And yet he could do better. What was there to lose?

'What you watching, son?'

Zak had been so immersed in the screen that he hadn't noticed his dad walk in the front door. He'd thrown his toolbox down on the floor and taken three short strides to the kitchen. The house wasn't big – two downstairs rooms and two upstairs rooms – but it was big enough for just the two of them. His dad picked up the scattered letters on the table and sighed as he read them.

'Good day at work?' Zak asked, turning quickly as if to show he had been fully aware of his surroundings. His dad snorted in response.

'Any day is a good day. It's not easy to get jobs with the

way things are at the moment. Nobody can afford to do any building work because of the recession. Still, on we go.'

Zak's dad hadn't always looked so defeated. Zak remembered a time when his mum was still in the house and his dad still had his regular work at the factory. Both of his parents were full of joy and excitement. Full of life. Zak had only been young when his mother was taken by illness, yet he hung on to the memories of her. His dad's joy had become desperation, and then, finally, acceptance. He couldn't change the past. He could only change the present, and that meant Zak. Zak knew he was lucky to have a father who cared for him. He came to watch every single match he played in, took him to every single training session, helped him to train in the back garden. They were a team.

'So what's this about?' he continued, pointing towards the screen. His hands showed a lifetime of manual work. They were firm, his arms muscular. Yet signs of his age were also starting to show. His hair was disappearing. His shoulders sagged. His whole appearance slightly crumpled.

Zak felt a thrill of excitement as he turned back to face the laptop as YouTube autoplayed the next Baller B video. They were a team when it came to football. Maybe they could also become a team when it came to shooting football videos.

'It's this guy called Baller B,' he explained. 'My mates at school told me to watch him.'

'Why? He's not very good.' Zak's dad gestured dismissively toward the screen. 'I've seen you do better skills in the garden.'

'Yeah, but do you know how much he earns?'

'As in, how much *money* he earns? This kid actually earns

money from this?'

'Dad, just look at the views. Millions of people watch this. Chris told me all about it. At first I didn't believe him, but then I searched online and he was telling the truth. Baller B earns millions of pounds every single year.'

'How can he do that?' Zak's dad looked genuinely confused. Social media was new to him. He'd only recently made his first Facebook page and seemed to use it only occasionally.

'Lots of different ways. YouTube pay you for getting views. Advertisers pay you. Fans pay you. Baller B is so popular he even has his own merch.'

'Merch?'

'Merchandise. Baller B snapbacks, hoodies, backpacks. Everything.'

'And people buy them?'

'Loads of them!'

It wasn't often that Zak's dad was lost for words. His eyes seemed to be operating outside his body, his cheeks puffed out in astonishment. Eventually, he regained his composure.

'Well, son,' he said. 'Why don't you give it a go then?'

3

The first warning sign came when Zak's dad tried to film him with the lens cover still on the camera. Once that was removed, he then managed to take a picture instead of a video. Chloe watched on in quiet amusement as Zak and his dad tried and failed to shoot a video in their back garden. The sun was still high in the sky, the clouds clear. For anyone else, it would have been an ideal condition to film in. 'Just back a bit more,' his dad requested.

'I can't go any further back!' Zak protested, raising his arms in exasperation, as if to show just how small the yard was. He was almost perched against the back wall of their yard. 'I told you we should have gone over to the park. There's no room here.'

'There's plenty of room. You and Chloe are always practising out here.'

'Yeah, Zak, stop finding excuses,' Chloe added from behind his dad. Dressed from head to toe in training kit, she absent-mindedly rolled her ball from foot to foot while watching on. The pair of them had a kickabout planned but that could wait. She was enjoying watching on too much.

'Well at least take down the washing line,' Zak said. 'I can't have your big pants appearing in my first ever video.'

'Okay, Zak. I think we're ready to rock and roll,' his dad announced from behind the camera, leaving the pants firmly on the line.

That was the cue.

In the background, Zak could see Chloe giving him a thumbs up. Finally, they were actually filming. Relieved yet nervous, Zak put a spring into his step as he approached the camera, doing his best to approach it from an angle that wouldn't show the pants.

'Yes, yes guys. This is Zak, and I'm going to be showing me some tekkers,' he said into the camera with all of the energy of Baller B.

'Stop!' his dad announced. Chloe's quiet amusement had turned into much louder amusement.

'Showing *me* some tekkers?'

Zak cursed himself and kicked the ball against the wall in anger. The camera was making him nervous. 'Let's go again,' he announced.

This time he got it right, proceeding to flick the ball up into the air with his heel. He readied his chest in anticipation, watching the ball carefully as it floated upwards. Only this time the ball didn't nestle onto his chest. Just like the red end of two magnets, the ball repelled itself from his body and bounced straight off.

'Argh!' Zak cursed himself again.

'Come on, Zak,' Chloe said from behind the camera. 'You do this all the time.'

She was right. He did do it all of the time. But usually he didn't have a camera pointing at him. The camera was making him think carefully about every single movement when usually he did everything naturally.

'Forget we're here,' his dad pointed out.

'Yes, fine,' Zak said in frustration, looking up to the sky and willing himself to perform as he knew he could. Once again he announced himself to the camera with plenty of energy, once again he flicked the ball with his heel. This time the control worked. The ball rolled to a halt on his chest and Zak held the pose for five seconds, knowing he was in perfect balance. Next up was the party trick: exactly the same as it had been in the playground. His body thrusted forward, the ball dropping to his right foot. Kick up, leg up, around the world. One, two, three. Ten times. He was in his flow. He was killing it. On the tenth around the world he kicked the ball into the small goal his dad had erected by the wall of the yard. 'Tekkers,' he winked to the camera.

'Awesome.' Zak's dad smiled with pride.

'Nice one,' Chloe added.

'Let's have a look,' Zak said as he raced over to the camera. His heart was pounding. He'd done it! Every skill nailed. It'd look good, he knew it. Already he could imagine it up on YouTube, his friends all liking and commenting.

'Oh,' his dad announced. 'How do you look at it?'

'Give it here,' Zak said. 'You need to press that button

that looks like play.' He pressed it and there he was, up on the camera's mini screen. 'Yes, yes guys,' he heard himself announce. There was room for improvement, that was for sure, but Zak noted that he looked full of energy, just like Baller B. The flick up with the heel – yeah, that worked well. Then the chest. Wait. Zak watched on the mini screen as the ball bounced off his chest.

'This isn't the right one!' he protested. 'Where's that one we just filmed?'

'Isn't it?'

'No! I didn't drop the ball, did I?'

'Not that I saw.'

'You did press record, didn't you?'

'Well, my memory is a bit fuzzy.'

Chloe could barely conceal her laughter. She bent over with her hands to her mouth, trying to make sure his dad didn't notice. Nothing could disguise that the last routine had been a waste. Nobody other than Chloe and his dad would ever see it. There was nothing else they could do but repeat it once more, this time with the camera on record.

On the sixth attempt, Zak finally managed to nail the routine. Immediately, his dad produced the proof that it had been recorded and they both breathed a sigh of relief. They'd done it.

'All right, thanks Dad,' Zak said. 'I'm going over the park to practise with Chloe. Tea in an hour, yeah?'

'That's right. Come back whenever though. I'll get this video put onto the computer in the meantime,' his dad replied. 'I'm going to try and do some editing.'

'As long as you don't delete it,' Zak pointed out before turning to Chloe. 'Sorry about that. I didn't think it'd take that long.'

'Don't apologise to me,' Chloe responded. 'That was a good laugh. Now, let's stop those seal tricks and do some proper practice, eh?'

'Good with me. I'm not sure I can face doing another take.' Zak smiled. He was looking forward to focusing on his training with Chloe. They had an important county cup game on the horizon for their team, Redwood Rovers. They'd both need to be at their best. Winning the county cup was the ultimate goal of any season. And maybe, just maybe, this would be their year.

4

Zak's tea lay cold and forgotten on the table. Fish fingers, beans and potatoes. Not the toughest of meals to cook but one of Zak's favourites. It was only upon seeing the lonely plate that the hunger hit him. All of that training had worked up quite an appetite. Two hours of passing, control and shooting, on top of his filming from before. The voice of his commanding Redwood Rovers coach, Mr Jones, came into his head as he greedily licked his lips. 'Food is the fuel for young footballers. Once you're low on fuel, you need to top up with top quality carbohydrates.' Well, top up he would. He placed the plate into the microwave and turned the dial to three minutes, hearing the reassuring buzz as the plate rotated slowly round and round. When he became rich and famous he'd pay some brainy scientist to invent an instant microwave. He hated having to wait for food.

A blitz of music startled Zak. He hadn't noticed his dad deep in concentration on the sofa, the laptop perched on his knees.

'Dad!' he exclaimed. 'I didn't notice you.'

'Oh, sorry son. I didn't hear you come in.'

As the music continued to play, the tune became recognisable. 'Gangnam Style' by K-pop artist PSY.

'Dad, why are you playing that stupid song?' Zak asked, chuckling to himself.

'Here, come over. Look at this.'

Intrigued, Zak moved to his dad on the sofa. There he was. On the screen Zak was juggling the ball. He watched on as he caught the ball on his chest, then worked it on to his right foot for the round the worlds. It felt surreal to see himself on the screen. Friends had always told him he was good at skills, but until now he'd never been able to see what his skills looked like from their viewpoint. Baller B had nothing on him. The thought made Zak smile. Until he realised why the music was playing.

'Have you put 'Gangnam Style' over my skills?!' he demanded, suddenly feeling a mixture of desperation and exasperation.

'What do you think, eh? Pretty rock and roll?'

'You are joking, right? Do you think someone like Baller B would have that cheese playing over his videos?'

'Well, maybe if he did he'd make billions rather than millions.'

'No, just no.' Zak didn't want to entertain his dad's suggestions. YouTube wasn't made for people his age. It was the pursuit of the young. The new generation's online voice. He could never understand. But then again, maybe he could. Because although the music selection was terrible, his editing job wasn't bad at all. He'd cut it at the right moments and had made Zak's voice clearer. 'It does look sick, though.'

'Thanks, son. I've visited a few online forums for some tips. I even watched some "how to" videos on YouTube.'

'Look, you see here.' Zak stopped the video just after his on-screen persona said showing you some tekkers. 'Right here we could add an explosion.'

'Why would you do that?'

'It gives the video energy. That's what Baller B does, anyway.'

'Well, if that's what you say. I think I did a tutorial on that.' He fiddled with a couple of buttons and sure enough a red ball of fire exploded on screen. 'Just let me add the sound.'

BOOM.

Yes, this was looking good. The microwave had long since pinged, yet Zak was now distracted. The pair sat in the dark, staring into the laptop screen. They watched the video through once more, this time without the background music.

'This is really good,' Zak commented, both surprised and satisfied at his earlier performance. All of those takes had been worth it in the end. Even the pants on the washing line had been edited out. Tremors of excitement were beginning to flit through his body.

'It is, son. Well done.'

'Now we just need a new song. What about that track by Dave? "Location".'

'I don't know that one.'

'Listen.' Zak took control of the laptop and browsed YouTube for the song. He clicked play and the music started up. Melodious. Bass pumping. Everything that PSY wasn't.

'It's a bit slow, isn't it?'

Zak sighed audibly. His dad was many things, but cool

wasn't one of them. 'It's cool. That's all that matters.'

'Well, if you're sure.' His dad clicked on a few more buttons and soon enough the new backing track was uploaded.

Now Zak was beyond excited.

They watched it once more, making sure the beat tied in with the movements. Perfect. They looked at each other, already in agreement. The excitement was also beginning to creep into his dad's face. Zak could see his mouth curving into a smile, the wrinkles in his cheeks deepening with the movement, his eyes twinkling.

'Shall we?' he asked.

'Let's get it uploaded,' Zak confirmed.

The red and white homepage of YouTube loaded onto the screen. In the top right corner, his dad clicked the create account button, then went through all of the essential steps. Email address. Password. Name.

'What should we call your channel?' he asked.

'Tekkers.' Zak's response was instant. He liked that name. It had a ring to it.

'Sorry, son. It's taken.' A red cross appeared next to the word that had been typed on the screen. 'What about adding your name?'

'Yeah, that makes sense. How about therealTekkerZak?'

'I like it. Why the real?'

'Because if I become famous, people need to know that it's the real me.'

'Whatever you say.' His dad typed once more into the keyboard and this time the red cross became a green tick. Account created.

'Get it uploaded, then!' Zak didn't want to waste another second. He was so excited that he wanted to see the video published now and not a second later. His dad clicked onto upload file, then dragged and dropped the edited video into the upload area. The loading banner crept up. 10%. 23%. Why was their WiFi so slow?

'We need to fill out all of these other details while it's loading,' his dad pointed out. 'Title. What about Introducing TekkerZak?'

'Nice. Let's get some hashtags into the caption. When I search for football videos I use hashtags to find new ones.'

'Okay then, what hashtags?'

'#Tekkers. #Football. #Skills. That should do.'

'Okay, well I think we're ready to rock and roll.' The loading banner had reached 100%, allowing them to press publish.

'Let's do it,' Zak said, his heart beating fast. Publish.

Zak took the laptop and watched the video again and again. He loved seeing the view count go up each time he watched it.

'What about your tea, Zak?'

'In a minute.' Zak's hunger had disappeared in the excitement. 'I just need to send some messages.'

'Okay, well make sure you eat it soon.'

Zak faked attention, just as he had done earlier in double science. His mind was nowhere near dinner. Instead, he grabbed hold of his iPhone 5 and opened WhatsApp.

Video up, c what u think. Youtube.com/watch=125tekkerzak

Message sent to Chloe. Then to their WhatsApp group with Chris, Josh and Marcus. They called it Redwood Legends. But why stop there?

Watch my new freestyle video. C what u think.
Youtube.com/watch=125tekkerzak

Send to all contacts.

Zak waited for the responses. Satisfied, he took hold once more of the laptop and watched his on-screen persona move the ball seamlessly around the screen. 'Tekkers,' he whispered to himself. The whole experience was beyond exciting. A beep on his phone. Quick, he had to grab it. Fear, excitement, his feelings were all over the place. This was the first response, the first time his online skills would ever be judged.

NEW SALE: PANTHER SPORTS TRAINING RANGE

Zak tossed his phone back to the sofa in disappointment. That wasn't the kind of notification he wanted.

Back to the laptop. Eleven views. Nine of them Zak. Again he clicked play, again he watched himself. Again and again, the buzz never quite leaving. Suddenly, his phone beeped. This time, it was a message.

CHLOE: Wicked

Typical Chloe, Zak thought. Her messages were always brief, economical. Yet he could always rely on his best mate. Another beep, another message, this one more expressive.

CHRIS: 🔥🔥🔥 love it man!

The movement was starting. Zak lay back on the sofa and hovered over the messages. His breathing was heavy. This was a rollercoaster. Would every video upload be like this?

'Zak, what are you doing son? You've got school in the morning.' Startled by the sound of his dad's voice, Zak dropped his phone onto the cushion and turned to see his dad halfway down the stairs, peering over the bannister in his dressing gown.

'I was just coming!' Zak insisted. It was only now that he noticed the time. 00:48. Talk about getting carried away! No wonder he'd only received a couple of messages in response. No wonder his view count hadn't gone up further. He took one final look at the screen – eighty-four views. Smiling, he closed the screen of the silver Dell Latitude. It was too late to eat now and anyway, the tiredness had hit him. His tea would remain cold in the microwave. Maybe he could have it for breakfast. Without helping it, his mouth opened in a cavernous yawn. Yes, he'd call it a night. He stood up and turned off the lamp beside the sofa. It was warm, the bulb his only companion for the past three hours. Darkness had long since fallen.

Tomorrow the views would come. The buzz would continue.

5

Eighty-five views. *Eighty-five.* How could only one person have watched the video since Zak last checked? Sunlight streamed into his bedroom through the open curtains. It was a beautiful day outside, the kind of spring morning that had birds singing in harmony while elderly neighbours tended proudly to their front gardens. Yet inside Zak's room all was not well. 08:15. He'd have to leave for school any minute. His green blazer was strung across the back of his chair, his trousers and tie crumpled on the floor. All around, posters of his idols looked down on him. Yet all of Zak's focus was on his phone.

'Zak!' he heard the cry from downstairs. 'Come on, you'll be late.'

He had to snap out of it, to try and put the disappointment to the back of his mind. The door rapped once, twice, and was then opened. Voices muffled before another cry travelled up the stairs.

'Chloe's here for you, son!'

Chloe. He really was late. He leapt out of bed and put his trousers on straight over his boxers. There was a green stain above the knee and a small hole in the thigh but it'd have to do. There was no time to find another pair. His crumpled blazer and shirt followed. The tie was stuffed into his school bag. That could be done in the playground. He checked his watch again. 08:19. Not bad.

'Make sure you have some breakfast,' his dad said as he charged down the stairs.

'Can you grab me a cereal bar, please? Oh, wait.' Zak turned on his heels and charged back upstairs. He'd almost forgotten his headband.

'Nice video,' Chloe said as soon as the pair left the house. 'Lucky your dad's pants didn't make the final cut.'

'Ha, yeah.'

'So are you a star yet?'

'Shut up.' He hadn't meant to say it so promptly. He'd meant to say it as a joke, but that wasn't how it came out.

'All right.' Chloe hit the brakes on her bike and locked her eyes on Zak. 'It was just a joke.'

'I know, I know.' He tore into his cereal bar. Maybe it was the lack of food or the lack of sleep. Maybe that was why he was feeling like this.

They rode to school in silence, Chloe going as fast as possible and Zak doing his best to keep up as usual. As they neared the traffic became heavier, almost impossible to pass in places. School buses blocked the roads before spitting out pupils in varying states of dress. 'Stainfield: tie!' Mrs Turnbull's voice cut through the laughter. 'Cassie, I can see that hoodie is not school regulation.' Once again, Zak's black trainers evaded her gaze. A small victory against authority.

The assembly hall was packed with year 8s. Despite the early hour, chatter filled the air. Zak fist-bumped and high-fived and hugged his mates as he saw them. They exchanged well-wishes and laughs, but few mentioned the video. Upon finding the rest of his form, Zak settled into an empty wooden chair next to Chris. Comfort was not one of Redwood Community College's strengths, but at least the chair was better than the floor.

'All right, Zak,' Chris said excitedly. Zak opened his mouth but Chris didn't bother waiting for an answer. 'I told you that you were better than Baller B, right?'

'Yeah, but I doubt Baller B only gets eighty-five views on his videos,' Zak shot back. Again, he couldn't help himself. His mouth acted before his brain processed the words to say. Still, Chris took it all in his stride.

'Eighty-seven actually. I just showed it to Marcus. Hey, Marcus.' Marcus had heard his name but didn't want to acknowledge Chris. He was deep in conversation with the girl next to him, Poorya, who everyone knew he'd fancied for months. 'So yeah, I didn't want to fight the guy. He was massive and in year 11 but he gave me no option. He hit me in the knee which is why I've got this plaster on but you should have seen the state I left him in.'

'Marcus!' Chris shook him as violently as you can shake a friend before it becomes unacceptable.

'What?' He turned around, visibly angry at being disrupted from his conversation with Poorya and his questionable memory of how he'd hurt his knee.

'The video.'

'Oh yeah, nice one Zak. I gave it a thumbs-up. I DM'd it to Josh too. I bet he'll like it.'

'Okay, great. Eighty-eight views once Josh watches it then.' Zak replied to the back of Marcus's head. His mate had already turned back to his conversation with Poorya. 'I don't think that's going to make me a millionaire.'

'You think Baller B's first video got a million views?' Chris laughed. 'Seriously, dude. That guy didn't go viral straight away. I've been watching him since early on but that stuff only got a few hundred views at most. Maybe a thousand. You just gotta keep grafting till you get lucky. If your videos are good then you'll get lucky eventually.'

'Yeah, yeah,' Zak said dismissively, looking into the crowd of faces.

'Serious.'

'But it takes so much time. I was up all night, first doing the video then helping my dad to edit and then putting it out.' Zak folded his arms. At least it hadn't been a costly mistake. He could deal with losing one evening.

'Just give it one more go,' Chris insisted. 'I'll spread the word round school. You know that I'm tight with the year 11s.'

'Tight as in they like to use you as their ball boy so they don't chase after their ball?'

'Exactly! We're tight. And once the year 11s start sharing your video you never know where it will end up.' Behind his square glasses, Chris's eyes were beaming. Zak could tell that his mate truly did believe in him. Sure, he exaggerated, but his face was expectant, hopeful.

'Fine, I'll give it another go.'

'That's it.' Chris put his arm around Zak and brought him close in celebration, rubbing his head in a half nuggy, half slap.

'Get off!' Zak complained, pushing Chris away. 'It's too early for all that.'

'It's never too early for a bit of rough and tumble. Honestly, I was just in this massive pile-on with all the year 11s only this morning.'

'Cool.'

'But yeah, enough of that. So you'll do another video tonight, yeah?'

'Tonight?'

'Yeah, go on. After all, it'll be good practice for our game tomorrow. Improve your control and all that. We're going to beat those farmers from their farmer league.'

'I don't think they'll be farmers. And just because the league is different to ours, it doesn't make it a farmers' league. Anything can happen in the county cup.'

'Anything can happen in anything,' Chris replied mysteriously, tapping his nose and winking.

'What does that even mean?'

'You'll find out.'

6

The more you work at something the better you become. Another of Mr Jones's pearls of wisdom floated into Zak's head as he stood once more in his back yard, his dad opposite him holding the video camera. Yesterday's video now stood at 146 views. News had travelled through the playground, but that news hadn't yet translated to views. Still, the increase in views had lightened Zak's mood to the extent that he was willing to listen to Chris and give filming another go.

Zak's Panther Sports shirt stuck to his chest as he went over his routine in the late afternoon sun. Sweat poured from the top of his forehead, pooling in above his black cotton headband. He wanted this to be a step up from the previous day. A more complicated routine was sure to be more impressive, which would be more likely to lead to more views.

'Are you ready yet, Zak?'

'Give me one more practice run.' He breathed heavily as he pinned all of his concentration on the ball. He flicked it up. A catch. A transition. An akka. One minute of pure tekkers. No mistakes. He was ready.

'Water,' he panted. 'I'm going to get some water, then let's film.'

'Right you are,' his dad said. 'I've got the camera all ready. No hiccups this time.'

Easier said than done.

'Yes, yes guys,' Zak said once more. He needed a catchphrase. It'd help him to stand out, to become memorable. 'It's Zak here again and I'm going to be showing you some tekkers.' In his mind he imagined the explosive boom that they'd edit into the video. Intro done. Now it was showtime. He backed up to the ball and thrashed it against the inside of his right foot. The ball looped up and he caught it between his heel and his bum. He held it for one second, two seconds, then flicked it up with his left heel. Only, he flicked the ball up too far. It looped over the fence and landed next door in Cyril's rose bush.

'Argh!' Zak screamed in frustration, kicking out against the air. He'd nailed that first set of skills.

'No worries, son,' his dad's voice carried across the back yard. 'If you could do it first time it'd be too easy. Best to film something properly challenging and get it right.'

'Yeah.' Zak was still stewing in frustration. He jumped the fence and retrieved the ball. Cyril was used to his regular jumps into the garden by now. Any anger he'd felt had long since evaporated over the years. He couldn't help it, so why fight it? Ball safely tucked under his arm, Zak vaulted the fence back into his garden.

'Give me a countdown,' he urged.

'All right. Three, two, one. Go!'

'Yes, yes guys. It's Zak here and I'm going to show you some tekkers.' The same again: the flick-up, the catch, the successful flick up to his head, where he rested the ball on his forehead. Slowly, he tilted his neck backwards so the ball followed the movement. It rolled slowly down his nose and stopped bang on the middle of his raised lips. His dad zoomed in as Zak kissed the ball, then rolled it back to his forehead, held the pose for another three seconds and then tilted his neck sharply forward so the ball snapped to stillness on the back of his neck. He loved that move. He knew it'd look great on camera. Almost there. He was close to finishing. All he had to do was his party trick of ten around the worlds, trap the ball dead on the floor and then do an AKKA 3000 into the empty goal. Only, wait. No, no, no! The ball had slipped from his neck. It was too late to recover. Gone. Zak had let his concentration wander for just a second but it was more than enough time to ruin what had been the perfect routine. Zak screamed in anguish once more.

'Calm down, Zak. You're going to make mistakes.'

His dad was speaking perfectly rationally. His words made perfect sense. But sense wasn't what Zak needed right now. He needed perfection.

Again they tried. Again they almost got there. The neck hold let him down once more. Back to the start. And again. And again. Zak became workmanlike in his movements. They'd taken too long now for the evening to be a waste. And then, finally, on the fifteenth take Zak managed it. He got to the AKKA 3000 and flicked the ball off his knee, moving it sharply right and following it with his right foot, with which he tapped the ball into the empty goal. Turning to the camera, Zak mouthed 'tekkers' and put his finger to his lips.

'Done,' his dad announced.

'YEEEEES! Get in there!' Zak jumped around the back yard. 'What about that Dad? That was sick. Mad. I'm buzzing!'

'It was good for sure. Well done. I don't even think we'll need to edit it much.'

'I'll give you that, that was sick.' Zak and his dad both turned to the gate where Chloe was standing, ball tucked under her arm. She might as well have had her own house key with how often she appeared from nowhere.

'I know,' Zak said, full of pride. All of those mistakes had been worth it. They had a video.

'Let's get it uploaded then,' his dad said, already walking back into the house.

'Can we do it later?' Zak knew that Chloe wouldn't want to wait around. Already she was moving her ball between her feet, itching to get down to the park to practise. 'It's just, we've got our game tomorrow and we wanted to do a few last bits of training.'

'Of course, son. I'll get the file onto the laptop and start editing it, how does that sound?'

'Perfect.'

'Good. And Chloe, do you still want a lift in the morning?'

'No, it's okay thanks Dean.' Chloe's voice was sickly sweet. Zak always admired how she was able to present herself around those older than her. 'My dad's giving me a lift. We'll see you there, though.'

'Right you will. And Zak, no wonder you're always hungry. Don't miss your dinner again tonight. I had to throw your fish fingers in the bin. You know what Mr Jones would say: food is fuel.'

'I won't, Dad. We'll just be an hour. Come on Chloe, race you to the park?' He was off before she could even respond, sharp on his toes, the wind brushing against his face as he left his best mate far behind.

7

Chicken and pasta: the perfect pre-match meal. Protein to build his muscles, carbohydrates to supply energy to his legs. Zak's dad had made him heat the meal up in the microwave before showing him what was on screen. Now, with the food steaming on his plate and knife and fork in hand, his dad placed the laptop next to him on the kitchen table.

'Hardly needed an edit,' he said, leaning back into the wooden chair next to Zak. 'Watch it through.' The click of the mouse's left button sounded and the video rolled into action on the screen. Feelings from yesterday came back. This still felt surreal. To see himself on screen. To see his true size in just the way others saw him, how the ball looked out of proportion nestled against his size 6 feet, how he moved around the screen, much more gracefully than he felt. If he blurred his vision, it could have been any freestyler. Well, not any freestyler, he thought as he watched the screen. The ball rolled from his forehead to his lips, then back to his forehead, always fully in control, always perfectly timed. Only the best of freestylers.

BOOM!

Another explosion had been added in for effect. A red fireball filled the screen, halting the thudding sound of the low bass track that had been put in as the backdrop sound. Zak had to hand it to his dad, he'd picked up the editing quickly.

'Yeah,' he said as the screen faded to black. 'Yeah,' this time with more certainty. 'I like it. No, I love it.'

'Well, that's good, because so do I.'

'Let's get it uploaded?'

'Yes.' His dad's hand moved the mouse around the screen with a confidence that would have seemed ridiculous just a couple of days ago. 'I've been having a little play around in the last day,' he explained, aware of Zak's eyes watching every movement. 'And after all, why not? It's new, it's exciting, and if all of your articles about Baller B are right, it might just make us a bob or two. Now, what should we call this one?'

'Sick routine from TekkerZak?'

'Okay, but I'm going to type it out like this.' The cursor bounced up and down in the blank box, moving further right with every letter.

SICK ROUTINE FROM TEKKERZAK !!

'It's louder, more energetic,' Zak's dad explained. 'Lots of the other YouTubers do it that way. It matches their on-screen energy.'

'You really have been reading up on it.' Zak was impressed. When his dad got excited about something, he truly did get excited.

'I had time on my hands,' he said in explanation. 'There was no work going on at the site today so I had to find something to do. I'd be surprised if I get any for the rest of this month.' No work again. Zak knew that he had less than most of his mates and didn't like to be reminded. He winced at the thought of his dad at home all day, curtains drawn, laptop open. At least he was doing something productive.

'And for the caption let's add the same hashtags as the last video. Then say Zak goes through a new routine.' He spoke quickly, trying to steer his dad away from the reminder of work.

'There's another thing I've learned,' he replied. 'Clickbait. Do you know what that is?'

'Nope.'

'It's a way of making people more interested in something so they are more likely to click it. So instead of saying what happens, we hint at what may happen. Watch this.' The cursor bounced up and down then moved left and right once more.

YOU'LL NEVER BELIEVE THIS CRAZY ROUTINE FROM TEKKERZAK!!

'I like it.' Zak nodded. 'What about the hashtags?'

'Good point.'

YOU'LL NEVER BELIEVE THIS CRAZY ROUTINE FROM TEKKERZAK!!

#TEKKERS #FOOTBALL #SKILLS

Yes, this really was looking good. A definite upgrade. A shiny package of tekkers, complete with clickbait and everything. His fingers tingled. He wanted the video uploaded now. Now.

'Go on then,' he said, trying to hide his excitement by scooping a pile of pasta. 'Publish.'

'Done.' The loading bar moved slowly along, its grey rectangle gradually taking up more of the screen. 'While we're at it, share it on your Instagram page. That way more people will see it.'

'Hardly anyone watched it after I messaged them yesterday,' Zak complained.

'If one person watches it who wouldn't have otherwise then that's good,' his dad pointed out. 'Ask them to share it and see what happens. I'll send it to my mates and put it out on my Facebook page too.'

'But you've got about ten friends on Facebook!'

'Ten more than nothing,' his dad shrugged.

This time round Zak didn't send the video to his whole contact list. He only sent it to those who had replied to his previous message. The others would be able to see it on his Instagram page.

Made a video and put it on YouTube! Check it out youtube.com/therealtekkerzak

That'd do. He clicked post and saw his video upload straight to the home page of Instagram. And then he waited.

Ten minutes. Four responses, all from the usual suspects: Chloe, Chris, Josh and Marcus. At least Marcus wasn't talking about his knee anymore. They were all in agreement that the new video was even better, the production definitely slicker.

At least some people liked it.

Zak yawned, a great big roar from the depths of his lungs. Lying on the sofa with his phone in his hands and laptop perched on his thighs, he suddenly felt the tiredness from his late night. Admittedly, the filming and training session with

Chloe probably didn't help. It couldn't detract from the buzz of putting himself out there online once more, because it really was a buzz. Showing the world your best and waiting for the world to respond was exciting. That was the beauty of the internet. Anybody could see him now: from the depths of the Amazon rainforest to the Great Wall of China. So long as they had WiFi.

There was the game to think of, though. He'd need a good night's sleep so he'd be refreshed and raring to go in the morning. Redwood simply had to win. Their semi-final exit from the county cup the previous season had been so painful. He didn't want to experience that pain again.

22:14. Time to call it a night. In bed he refreshed the YouTube app on his phone to see that the new video was up to forty-five views. Worse than yesterday. He wanted to succeed, to get millions of views. But he really wanted to play well the next day. And so he went to bed dreaming not of views, but of goals.

8

'Zak! Wake up, you're never going to believe this!'

'Wheurgh.'

As far as Zak was concerned, the morning was for sleeping. Getting up early every day for school was an inconvenience. Only on a matchday did he happily leave the comfort of his bed nice and early. And even then it took him a long time to adjust to being fully awake. Now he tried to focus. There was a blurred figure standing above him. Who was it? It had to be his dad, didn't it? That's right. There were the posters of Abou Trabt. The football trophies. The sky blue walls. He was definitely in his bedroom. He reached up and rubbed his eyes, feeling the unmistakeable touch of human contact. Yes, he was awake. But wait, what? The contact wasn't just from his own hands. His whole body was being shaken.

'Wheurgh . . . wheurgh you doin'?' he complained, trying and failing to speak as clearly as his alertness would allow him to.

'Look, just look.' A bright phone screen was shoved into his face. Zak blinked at the brightness. His eyes weren't yet ready for such harsh light. Creasing his face he squinted, trying to make out the screen. A red banner. Rectangle. White background. YouTube. He squinted harder. It was him! His video. For a few seconds he admired the on-screen Zak as he completed his seventh, eighth and ninth around the world. 'Look at the views!'

He was still being shaken. Couldn't his dad have waited until breakfast? At least he could have got a bit more sleep that way.

Wait.

The views.

More than forty-five.

Much more.

15,781.

Maybe he was still dreaming?

He grabbed a sliver of skin between the nails of his thumb and index fingers and pinched. A sharp flinch of pain spread out from the area he was holding. Looking back at the screen, the number was still there. 15,781. He took hold of the phone, disbelievingly snatching it from his dad and scrolling further down the screen.

1,241 thumbs up.

17 thumbs down.

143 comments.

452 subscribers.

Suddenly he was more awake than ever before. His eyes flitted up, down, left and right, taking in the information on the screen. Such big numbers. How had it happened? His video had actually meant something to people. They'd watched it, enjoyed it, commented on it and shared it with their friends. A check of the comments section revealed as much.

'TEKKERZZZ' @2muchsauce

'THIS KID IS UNREAL' @smithy12345

'TO DO THAT . . . THEN HIT TOP BINS!' @ronaldo_ superfan

'YO THIS GUY HAS A BIG FUTURE' @2muchtekk

Madness. He'd shown the world his best and the world had responded, just like he always hoped but never truly expected it would. Delirious, startled, happiness radiating from every inch of his body, he passed the phone back to his dad and then reached to the side of the bed where his own phone had been flung the night before. He pressed down on the top button to wake the screen. Hundreds of notifications jumped out at him. Messages from friends he hadn't spoken to in months, DM requests from unknown accounts, new likes, followers and shares. He opened Instagram to find his follower count had tripled to 390. WhatsApp was similarly buzzing.

Told u anything can happen, Chris had messaged with a sticky-out tongue face. How right he was.

'Son,' the familiar voice sounded and a tender hand was placed on his shoulder. 'I think you're on to something here.'

'I think you're right,' Zak replied, a broad grin plastered across his face.

How relieved he was to have given the video a second go. How happy that he'd been talked round. This, this is how Baller B must have felt after every upload. No, hundreds of times better than this. If 15,781 views felt this good then how good must a million feel? His eyes remained glued to the screen, his thumb pressing and holding up, then down, to refresh the pages. Each time, the numbers got bigger. Still, his body was shaking but this time shaking all by itself. His arms, legs, everything, all shaking with the energy coursing through him. It was enough to make him feel that he could do anything. Run a marathon, swim the Channel, win the county cup.

'Now, come on. Get up and get dressed,' his dad reminded him. 'You've got a game to win. You cereal is on the table. So is the orange juice. I've cleaned your boots for you, make sure you pack everything else in your bag. We're leaving in 45 minutes. Don't be late.' With that he was gone, leaving Zak alone with his phone and his thoughts. In that moment, there was nowhere else that he would rather have been.

YouTube subscribers: 561
Instagram followers: 390
Twitter followers: 156

'Here he is, our new celebrity!'

Redwood Rovers FC clapped and cheered as Zak opened the faded wooden door and walked into the whitewashed portacabin that acted as their home changing room. The noise bounced around the four walls, teammates standing on the benches and blocking from sight Mr Jones's detailed set-piece diagrams that had been pinned all around them.

'Settle down, settle down,' said Mr Jones, trying to restore some order to his team. He checked the clipboard clutched against his muscular chest and then blew sharply on the whistle that was hanging around his neck. 'I said settle down! Now, Zak, your shirt is in the usual place. Hurry up, everyone else is almost ready.'

When Mr Jones told you to hurry up, you hurried up. If the ever-present clipboard, the whistle or the tightly sculpted muscles didn't give it away, then the close-cropped haircut, tucked-in t-shirt and insistence on referring to him as Mr Jones certainly did: Mr Jones was a man of discipline. He'd spent several years in the army during his early twenties before joining Redwood Rovers as a full-time coach and club secretary. For the footballers of Redwood, Redwood Rovers meant Mr Jones and Mr Jones meant Redwood Rovers.

A couple of teammates fist-bumped Zak as he scuttled to his usual spot next to Chloe, keen not to get on Mr Jones's wrong side.

'What took you so long?' she whispered.

'Sorry, things were a bit mad this morning.' Sensing his best mate's tone, Zak decided it was best to scoot over what had really happened. Things were more than just a bit mad. Once his dad had left him to get ready, Zak lay transfixed to the screen, scrolling over and over through the comments, refreshing the page until his dad had to come and physically pick him out of bed. He'd rushed through the bathroom, clubbed together his Redwood Rovers tracksuit and poured himself a bowl of cornflakes and a glass of orange juice which he then had to delicately balance on his lap in the car as they sped through the streets of Redwood.

'Hmm.' Chloe's gaze didn't try to hide the fact that she wasn't convinced. Her eyebrows were raised in expectation that Zak would tell her the real reason any second. 'It wasn't because of your video, was it? Because that was amazing and I'm so happy that it's gone viral. But that doesn't matter right now. Make sure you focus on the game today. If we win this, we go through to the next round of the county cup.'

The county cup. The biggest test that Zak and his teammates would face all season. Teams from far and wide, all attempting to be named the best in the county so they would qualify for the national championships. Zak nodded to her. This was serious. Despite all of the morning's madness, he had to try and put thoughts of internet fame out of his mind. Right now, Redwood had a game to win. If they were going to win it, they'd need Zak to be at his best.

'You're in your normal position, Zak,' said Mr Jones as he reached for his usual number 10 shirt. 'Up front with Chloe. I want us to keep possession of the ball, but if you get the chance to shoot then make sure you have a go.'

'Yes, Mr Jones,' Zak said with a nod. Mr Jones smiled. He liked it when his players referred to him as Mr Jones. He felt it gave them discipline, and if any player was to make it as a professional then they'd certainly need discipline.

'Good,' Mr Jones replied. 'Once you've got your boots on get everyone out for a warm-up. I'll meet you at the side of the pitch.' With that he turned on his heel and left the changing room. He liked it when his players led their own warm-up. He felt it gave them discipline.

As soon as the door closed the changing room erupted into noise which was anything but disciplined. All of the players had their pre-match routines. Although Chloe liked to sit quietly and visualise what she was going to do on the pitch, her teammates were much louder. Marcus and Josh liked to practise their celebration handshakes while cheering as loudly as possible (even though neither of the defenders had ever scored a goal). Chris liked to talk to whoever would listen, which, this morning, meant Zak. And Zak liked to go around the whole team and high-five every single one of them – once he'd thanked Chris and heard just how Chris had got all of the year 11s to share the video and that was probably why it had so many views.

'Come on,' he yelled at the top of his voice after moving Chris to one side. 'Today is our day!'

Every high-five became more energetic. Every player became more enthused. By the time he'd done his round the whole team was brimming with excitement.

But the game started evenly. Redwood's opponents, Barton Town, were an unknown quantity. While Redwood played in the North Moors league, Barton Town were in the South Moors league. They only ever met in the County Cup. From looking at their league table, Zak knew that Barton Town were one of the better teams in their division, currently sitting in fifth place. Good, but not as good as Redwood's current unbeaten record. Rovers hadn't lost all season and played with the confidence that came from so many victories. They passed the ball around the pitch at pace, prodding and probing at their opponents. Barton were happy to sit back and soak up the pressure. Try as they might, neither Chloe nor Zak could find any space in Barton's compact defence.

Zak made his usual runs. He occupied his usual positions. But everything that he did seemed to be half a second too slow. No matter how hard he attempted to concentrate on the game going on all around, flashes from that morning shot into his mind. Internet fame. Views. The rush. No, he had to snap out of it. Focus. Suddenly the ball was at his feet, but just as quickly it was whisked away again by a Barton defender. That didn't usually happen.

'Come on Zak,' roared a figure from the crowd. 'Play your game, son.' Zak could see his dad in his usual position, right by the halfway line. Next to him was a reporter from the local newspaper, *The Redwood Review*, furiously making notes into a battered notebook.

'Too easy.' The Barton defender who had robbed him of possession had jogged back into position after playing a pass forward. Right next to Zak. He could feel the defender's stale breath on the back of his neck, sense his lanky presence. 'You should stick to making videos. At least then you don't have anyone trying to get the ball off you.'

Zak knew he should be angry. Nobody told him he was no good at football. But at the same time, he was shocked. This defender had *seen* his video. He'd actually seen his video. Not only that, but he knew who Zak was. Zak turned to face his tormentor. He had small, grey eyes with an outbreak of spots across his cheeks and a smirk inked into his face.

'You've . . . seen my video?' Zak asked. The defender laughed to himself and quickly darted off.

'Zak!' yelled Chris. 'I can't keep making passes if you're not going to chase them.' So that was why his tormentor had darted off. The defender with the spots was now on the edge of his penalty area, turning with the ball that was intended for Zak.

'What's wrong with you?' Chloe demanded as the ball was

lofted back toward Redwood's defence. 'You only get one chance in the cup. Let's not waste it.'

She was right. He would only get one chance. If they failed to win, their cup run would be over for another year.

Zak shook his head, adjusted his armband, and took a deep breath. 'Come on,' he told himself, 'you can do this.'

'Stop talking to yourself and start playing,' said Chloe, now standing within ten yards of him. Beads of sweat dripped down her forehead and onto her pink cheeks. 'I can't win the game by myself.'

Start playing. He had to start playing. Get the ball and do what he always did. Prove that lanky idiot wrong and show his talent. Forget internet fame. Forget his rushed preparation. Snap out of his sluggishness. Suddenly the ball was at his feet. He sensed his tormentor approaching from behind and shifted his body weight left, then moved the ball right. It worked. The defender moved left, earning Zak a yard of space, twenty yards from goal. He looked up and saw the keeper in her goal, saw the target, and drew back the laces of his golden Panther Sports boots before letting fly with his weaker left foot. The shot was far from his best – straight at the keeper with no real power – but it was at least a shot on target, a small victory over his tormentor. He was in the game.

And so were Barton. Marcus, playing with an entirely unnecessary bandage over his right knee, was forced into a slide tackle that grazed his other knee but stopped a certain goal. Their opponents were growing in confidence, no longer just sitting back but also willing to launch their own attacks. In desperation, Zak found himself charging around his own half more often, either in search of possession or trying to stop an attack. The half-time whistle, when it came, was a relief to them all. They had been on the back foot.

Mr Jones gathered his team into a tight circle on the side of the pitch, making sure they each had their bottle of water with them. Hydration, he always told them, was key. If they had enough water in their body, they'd have more energy for the final ten minutes of every match. Zak greedily gulped his water down. He'd certainly need energy.

'You need to give me more, Zak,' Mr Jones announced. 'That was promising at the end, but Chloe's having to work so hard at the moment. Match her work rate, then we'll start to see success.'

'Yes, Mr Jones.'

'And don't worry. We have time. Forty-five minutes is a long time in a game of football and I know you're the better team. You just need to prove it.'

They ran back onto the pitch with renewed energy, hungrily awaiting the referee's whistle to restart the match. When it came, the match ebbed and flowed once more, the ball zipping around the pitch with all of the intensity that comes from a knockout cup tie. One second it was Josh making a last-ditch tackle to prevent a certain Barton goal, the next it was Chloe striking the post. As the game raged around him, Zak began to get more touches of the ball. He started simple, controlling with the instep, scanning the pitch and finding the best pass available. As more of his passes came off, his confidence grew. His tormentor wasn't getting a kick. The thought made Zak smile. Now it was time to prove him wrong.

Zak dropped into his half in search of the ball. Josh obliged, passing it forward from defence. Zak checked his shoulder before receiving the ball and saw he had room to turn. Just. A defender was bearing down on him but was running at him square on. Instinctively, he nudged the ball forward with the studs of his boot. The defender hadn't expected that. He just had time to call 'Megs!' before retrieving the ball after it had travelled through the defender's legs and driving forward. Now the pitch was opening up. Another defender charged and this time he touched the ball to the right and then just as quickly moved his foot to the outside of the ball and cut it back inside with the instep. A flip-flap. Another defender beaten. He could sense the roars of the crowd, the feeling that his game had just gone up a level.

'That's more like it, son!' his dad exclaimed on the side. 'Show 'em what you got!'

But Zak didn't notice him. All of his attention was on the game. Chloe had peeled off to the right wing, no more than thirty yards from goal. She'd seen the space between the right back and centre back, and now so did Zak. He threaded a pass with the outside of his right boot. It looked to be heading straight for the centre back, but then curved in the air, perfectly dissecting the two defenders. Chloe raced onto the bouncing pass and touched it into her path with a delicate thigh. She swung back her right foot and then smashed it forward, connecting with the ball right in its centre. The ball flew through the air, the keeper flew through the air, her fingers outstretched. She'd done enough. The ball flicked against her fingers and deflected over the bar for a corner kick. 'Ooh!' the crowd groaned, a mixture of disappointment and relief depending on who they were supporting, before applauding the all-round display of football: great save, great attacking play.

Chloe joined in with the applause to show Zak her appreciation. Feeling ten feet tall, he jogged to take the corner, waves of confidence running through his body. It was down to him to deliver set-pieces. The target was obvious. Josh and Marcus had come up from defence and now prowled the area, excited at their chance to come forward. Zak lofted the ball toward them, hitting it below the valve so that it floated straight. Marcus was first onto it, sensing its flight before anyone else. He gave his opponent a slight nudge then took two, three, four steps forward and propelled himself into the air, his arms used as the levers to lift him above all others in the area. The ball met him smack on the forehead and he tensed his neck muscles to add even more power. The keeper never stood a chance. Marcus's header powered past her before she could even raise an arm.

'YEEEEEES!' Zak screamed, running to try and catch Marcus as the feeling of elation took hold. The Redwood supporters screamed in delight, their substitutes running onto the pitch in the hope of joining in the celebrations. Ecstatic, Marcus was beating his chest and screaming at the top of his voice. Nothing, ever, anywhere would ever beat the feeling of scoring a goal. Not for anyone.

The one-goal lead forced Barton to attack more. They pushed forward in a sea of blue, but in doing so left spaces in their backline. Zak skulked around the pitch, every step taken in the anticipation that he was only ever seconds away from creating a second goal for his team. With every touch of the ball he felt an opportunity. Barton's defence did their best to shackle him, Zak's tormentor following his movements. If he could just get that second goal, they'd almost be through.

A Barton attack. A brave tackle. The ball played upfield to Zak on the counter attack. Defenders charged and he ducked and dived past them. A roulette around the first defender, stopping the ball with his right foot and then swivelling 180 degrees with his left, a double stepover past the second. A one-two with Chloe, but the second pass was cut out and now Barton were on the attack once more. 'Come on,' Zak willed his defenders. 'Hold out.' The referee checked his watch, then checked it again. There couldn't be long left. As the ball was cleared to safety once more, several of Barton's players put their hands on their knees and took gulps of breath. They were close to running on empty. On the sideline, the collection of friends and parents sensed the game was nearing its end. Those supporting Barton roared in support, urging their players forward, while the rest urged Redwood to hold on.

Time does funny things to people. In football, they abandon all of their strategies that have worked so well and become desperate. And so it was that Barton bombarded Redwood's box, launching high balls in the hope of winning the header. But Josh and Marcus, playing in the heart of the defence, were equal to everything. 'Away!' they screamed with each header. The slick passing game Mr Jones preached had long since been abandoned. Anywhere would do, as long as the ball wasn't near Redwood's goal. Clearances continued to be thumped in the general direction of Barton's goal. And then, finally, one came in Zak's direction. Marcus had kicked it with all of his might and the ball sailed into the right channel. Barton had thrown all but two defenders forward in their desperation for a goal, leaving themselves exposed. Recognising an opportunity, Zak pumped his arms back and forth and catapulted his legs forward. The lanky defender, sensing the danger, charged in the same direction. He had a headstart, just ten yards from the ball, but Zak was fast. He was closing in on the ball, his golden feet blurring across the ground. Fifteen yards. Ten. Five. He drew alongside the defender who flung an elbow in Zak's direction. It was aimed at his face but the aim was poor, thudding against his chest. Air escaped from Zak's lungs as the force of impact slowed him. They were running at the same speed now, the ball rolling slowly, ever closer toward Barton's goal.

Too easy.

The defender's words played over in Zak's mind. He'd show him. He'd prove him wrong. And with that he forgot about the quickly darkening bruise on his chest. He pushed against the ground with as much force as was physically possible. Suddenly he was ahead of the defender, the ball in sight. Recognising defeat, the defender lunged at Zak in a vicious slide tackle but Zak had been expecting it. He jumped over the leading leg, missing it by millimetres, and took control of the ball. The white line marking the edge of the penalty area flashed beneath his feet and he realised he was in Barton's area. The goalkeeper approached, narrowing the angle from which Zak could shoot to make the goal appear as small as possible. He looked up, assessed the keeper, looked at the defender desperately trying to get back to stop the attack, drew his right foot back to shoot – and then saw Chloe. She'd gone undetected, sprinting forward and calling for the ball. The goalkeeper hadn't seen her, the defender couldn't catch her. The goal was at her mercy.

'Square it!' she screamed. 'I'm free!'

Zak moved his right foot forward. The keeper planted her feet, ready to dive either side to save the ball. The defender screamed in anguish. His foot was centimetres from the ball now. And then, at the last instant, Zak twisted his body. Instead of smashing the ball into the awaiting keeper, he played it across the area.

The defenders hadn't expected it. The goalkeeper hadn't expected it. But Chloe had. She happily accepted Zak's gift and swept the ball into the open goal.

The crowd erupted. Mr Jones erupted. The players erupted. Even the reporter's notebook and pen were lost in the madness of hugs and fist-bumps and hair ruffles and high fives. Redwood Rovers were 2-0 ahead.

'Great assist,' Chloe smiled at Zak through the tangle of bodies.

'Hey,' Zak responded coolly. 'It was no sweat.'

'No sweat? That was the sweatiest goal I've ever seen!' laughed Chris.

'It doesn't matter,' said Zak. 'There's nothing wrong with sweaty goals. Especially when they put us through to the next round of the cup.'

As Zak made the joyful slow jog back to his position for the kick-off he lingered in front of the lanky defender. The defender's small grey eyes were cast down, refusing to look at Zak. Too easy. Zak smiled at the thought. There was no point in getting involved in stupid battles. He'd just let his feet do the talking, like always.

'Come on, number 10. Back to your half. The whistle is going in thirty seconds.'

Not yet, Zak thought. He wanted to saviour this moment. The best thing that had happened all day.

YouTube subscribers: 924
Instagram followers: 610
Twitter followers: 215

How did they make all the trees so perfect? On Glenn Close, everything was in absolute symmetry. The trees all reached the same height, their leaves the same colour, their branches clipped to the millimetre, birds nestled in their nooks and crannies and tweeting in blissful harmony. The smattering of self-satisfied houses, made from modern brick and crafted from the latest building methods, sat in their own areas of paradise. Front gardens of carefully tended flower beds releasing the freshest of smells, driveways with two cars and preened front lawns hinting at the riches inside. This was the same town that Zak lived in, but it was a million miles from his reality. He looked longingly at the buildings, thought of the happy families that lived in each one. The feelings were always the same, no matter how many thousands of times he visited. In a happy vision of the future he'd live in one of these houses, happy with his own family, known worldwide as one of the very best footballers. Well, he smiled, at least he was part of the way to being recognised for his football skills.

In such surroundings, Chloe's house stood out. Not so much because of the house itself, because like all of the others it was four bedrooms, detached and spacious. No, Chloe's house stood out because of the grass. There was surely a time when it had been green, perhaps before the Smiths moved in. Chloe and her younger sister Clare had soon seen to that. No amount of gardening could repair the practice spots that Chloe chose. Scuffed up from her kicks and turns and footsteps, the Smiths' front garden was spotted with signs of use. The garage wall, separated from the rest of the house, was marked with targets. Chips of fence were missing from rogue strikes. It was a house that screamed of life, rather than the perfect symmetry of all the others in the cul-de-sac.

Zak dumped his bicycle in the front garden and rapped twice on the oak door. He was fine to leave it there. It wouldn't be stolen on Glenn Close. There was no sign of life on the cul-de-sac and even if there was, they wouldn't want his bike. The door jerked back on its hinges and Mrs Smith answered the door with a smile, just as she always did when she saw that it was Zak knocking. A waft that smelt of home baking hit Zak. Mrs Smith brushed off her apron as if in explanation. Everything about her was homely, from her reassuring nature to her constant contentment and gentle encouragement. She didn't talk so much as sing when she spoke.

'Well hello, Zak. Well done yesterday – what a super result!'

'Thanks, Mrs Smith. It was a great game. Is Chloe in?' Zak loved his friendly welcomes from the Smiths. He was around their house so much that he was practically part of the family. Zak's dad always said he was like the son the Smiths had never had.

'Chloe,' Mrs Smith sung up the stairs. 'It's Zak here for you, darling.'

'One minute,' came the distant reply. Mrs Smith turned back and smiled once more at Zak. He never knew why, but Zak always went a little red when Mrs Smith smiled at him.

'Do come in. How's your dad getting on?'

'Good, he's good, thanks.'

'Oh, I am glad to hear it. I do sometimes worry about him since. . .' Mrs Smith tailed off, as if unsure where to go with her sentence.

'He's fine,' Zak burst out, a little too quickly. The past was the past. The painful, unchangeable past. A shiver ran through Zak's spine and he could tell that Mrs Smith regretted her previous words. Her mouth contorted into an circle, as if silently saying 'oh'.

'All right, Zak?' Chloe came down with a huge grin on her face, much to the relief of both Zak and Mrs Smith. 'Feels great to still be in the cup, eh?'

'You know it.' The pair fist-bumped.

'Kickabout?' Chloe asked. She was already dressed in her training kit, hair already tied up in a ponytail.

'You know it.'

'There'll be muffins for you after, darlings,' Mrs Smith sung after them as they slammed the front door shut. 'Blueberry.'

It was always the same ritual at the weekend. Sometimes at Zak's house, sometimes at Chloe's. Sometimes it'd even be in the park or down the rec. But it was always the same. The two would meet up and practise their skills together for a few hours. Then it was time for a lunch of a couple of sandwiches and a few games of *FIFA*. After that the pair would go off in search of a proper game with their teammates and friends from school, usually Chris, Josh and Marcus, or even just with anyone else kicking around in the park. And that was just the way they liked it.

Today was a park day. Chloe wanted to work on her fitness and though the back garden at her house was big, it wasn't big enough to run 100 metre sprint intervals. And Zak's back yard certainly wasn't.

Despite it being mid-morning, much of Redwood was still yet to wake up. The streets were quiet, quiet enough for the pair of them to pass the ball back and forth between each other along the road, sharply returning to the pavement at the sound of the odd car driving at a little over the 30-miles-per-hour limit. Dog walkers clutched on to their leads and their poop bags, the same ones raising their hands in acknowledgement to Zak and Chloe that always did so. At the church they turned right onto Upper Street. Men and women trickled from Bill's newsagents with their Sunday papers – the same as always – while parents hurriedly ushered their children into church, well aware from the dong of the ringing bells that they were already late for Reverend Johnson's service. No matter how much the outside world changed, Zak knew that Redwood would stay just the same. A hundred years from now people would still be hurrying toward the church's big oak doors, dog walkers would still be rubbing the sleep from their eyes as their bulldogs and greyhounds roamed the streets, customers would still emerge from their red brick houses to ding the door of the newsagents. The familiarity was reassuring. Yes, Zak wanted excitement. Chloe wanted excitement. All of them wanted excitement. But at the same time, the dull town life was a comfort.

'So, fitness today,' Chloe announced. 'I felt myself flagging early on in the game yesterday. But I suppose I was having to do all of your running for you.' She playfully punched Zak in the arm.

'No wonder the others didn't want to join us! You keep on doing my running for me and I'll keep on putting those passes on a plate for you,' Zak retorted, pulling Chloe in close to him. 'You can thank me for your goal.'

'Yes, it was nice of you to start playing in the second half.' She escaped Zak's clutches. 'I wouldn't have minded you sticking about in the first half rather than just daydreaming about that video.'

Zak shrugged his shoulders. She had a point. At first he had struggled to put the thoughts of internet fame to the back of his mind. He'd have to deal with that better in future matches. But he didn't want to have to admit that to Chloe. Best to change the conversation. 'So how long are we training for today?'

'Well, it's the day after the game so we shouldn't practise for too long. I don't want to do too much and risk an injury. I just need to do some sprints to get my speed endurance up. I don't want to get tired early on again in the next cup match. We need to keep getting better if we're going to win it this season.'

'An hour then?'

'An hour.'

The park was a hundred metres down the road on the right, a single worn pitch surrounded by trees and a soft-play area. Toddlers and their parents dotted the soft play area but the pitch remained empty. While Zak dumped their water bottles and ball by the goalpost, Chloe measured a spot thirty paces from the goalmouth and marked it with her jumper. For the next forty-five minutes they took turns sprinting to the marker and back. While one ran, the other rested, then after ten goes each they took a long rest before going all over again.

Gulping fresh air into his lungs, Zak pounced at his water bottle as soon as his sprints were over. The burn in his calf muscles told him that he was working hard, which meant that the training was working. If he wanted to get better, he'd have to work hard.

'10,000 hours,' Chloe knowingly pointed out after downing half of her own bottle.

'You what?'

'I read it in a book. There was this study that found that if you want to become an expert at anything you need to practise it for 10,000 hours.'

'That's mad.'

'It sounds mad, but over ten years it works out at three hours a day.'

'That is mad!' Zak protested.

'But do it over twenty years and that's only ninety minutes a day. That's not much. Especially when you consider that footballers are at their best around 28 or 29.'

'So we're going to become world class sprinters then, doing this?' Zak enjoyed winding Chloe up. He knew that training their speed endurance was important to help them play at their best for longer in a match. It was just more fun to act ignorant. Chloe clocked him. She knew him well enough to know when he was faking ignorance and instead chose to ignore him. 'Best get practising then,' Zak winked, reaching out for his ball and flicking it up with his heel. He'd spent the morning scouring the internet for new tricks and now seemed the perfect time to try them. At the very least they might wind up Chloe. At the very best, he'd nail them quickly and use them in his next videos. That was what he needed to do if he was going to become a top YouTuber. His followers would want to see new things. His content would have to remain fresh. And the only way to perfect those new tricks was in training.

Zak cursed as a particularly tough routine that he'd seen @seanfreestyle landing, involving raising his arms together in a diamond shape and spinning his body around as fast as possible to move the ball around the raised arms, left him dizzy and the ball in the bushes. That was the problem with new tricks: they were never easy at first.

'That's hardly going to be useful in a game, is it?' Chloe pointed out.

'We'll see,' Zak winked.

'I mean, it looks cool,' Chloe continued. 'Or it would do if you didn't keep on dropping the ball. But what's the point?'

'What's the point? To make people happy.' Chloe wrinkled her nose at Zak. She wasn't buying it and suddenly Zak realised that it wasn't him winding her up, but her winding him up. She was starting to get to him, but unlike her he couldn't just ignore it. 'People all around see my skills,' he continued, a little faster, a little more forceful. 'They watch and want more. And that's not to mention the money people make from it. Baller B makes millions and he's not even that good at skills!' That'd show her.

'Have you made any money from it yet?'

'I've only just started!'

'Seems like a waste of time. You couldn't pay me to freestyle instead of actually play.'

'That's easy for you to say,' Zak shot back, picturing her big house, her happy family life, the way her parents could get her anything she wanted. His attack had backfired. He was defensive, angry even.

'Well, it's true.' Chloe folded her arms. She wasn't budging.

'You wouldn't understand,' Zak muttered. And he was right. She wouldn't understand. Nobody could understand the rush that he had felt. The thrill of recognition, of likes, of followers. Not if they'd never experienced it themselves. The thrill had been so powerful that he wanted more. Especially with the county cup game safely won.

'Whatever,' Chloe moved on quickly. 'Fancy a bite? Come on, let's go to mine. Best of five on *FIFA*?'

It was best to leave their disagreement. Zak nodded and followed his best mate out of the iron park gates, back to the other world of Glenn Close.

The smell of muffins hit him as he entered the grand oak door. 'Shoes!' Mrs Jones scolded them, rushing from the kitchen to the front door. 'Take them off. Me and your dad already spend our lives picking up mud from this house.'

68

'I was just taking them off!' Chloe complained.

'Well make sure you were. Hello again, Zak,' her voice transformed instantly as she beamed in his direction. 'Come in and have a muffin. You can stay for lunch, too.'

As Zak bit into his freshly-made blueberry muffin while falling into the cushions of the Smiths' pearl grey corner sofa, he felt truly content. Mrs Smith was a brilliant baker. The textures melted together in his mouth, light and airy, the blueberry perfectly added.

'Here you go.' Chloe handed him the Xbox controller he always used – the one with the official FC Barcelona skin, the left half of the joypad maroon and the right half blue with the Barcelona badge. She always used the Real Madrid controller. Zak put his muffin to one side and dragged himself up. He played better when he sat forward in his chair, and right now he wanted to sit as far forward as possible. When it came to *FIFA*, every game against Chloe was the ultimate battle. He hated to lose, but he'd hate it even more after her words from earlier in the park. He'd made a point of grunting his responses to her on the walk back, showing he was annoyed at her. How he'd love to beat her now.

He selected Barcelona, she selected Real Madrid. He went with a 3-4-1-2, Lionel Messi in the creative number 10 role. But the opening of the game was all Real Madrid.

'And just like yesterday, Chloe Smith goes charging on the counter attack,' Chloe commentated. On the screen his pixelated player was desperately trying to track back. No matter how hard he pressed his controller, the player wouldn't move fast enough. 'And just like yesterday, Zak Oxden is nowhere to be seen.' She was in his penalty area now, controlling Karim Benzema. Zak held the Y button and the virtual ter Stegen reacted, charging to the danger.

'Don't do it,' he warned Chloe, noticing Eden Hazard running parallel to the action, the empty net wide open. 'Don't do it.'

'Watch me.' Just before shooting, the virtual Benzema passed the ball sideways, for the virtual Hazard to score. 'Ha!' Chloe laughed.

'Not cool,' Zak retorted. 'No sweaty goals allowed on this game. It's too easy to square it for an open goal. You should only be allowed to score sweaty goals in real life.'

'Hey, I'll do whatever I've got to do,' Chloe laughed. 'It doesn't matter anyway. You're probably still thinking about that video. How many people have watched it now?'

The video was a dangerous conversation. Chloe had already got to him that morning. But here was a chance to get back at her, to prove that she was wrong and he was on to something. Zak played up to the question, umming and ahhing as if he hadn't constantly been monitoring the numbers ever since getting back home from the cup game. 'Around 25,000,' he eventually said.

Chloe almost spat out the sip of water she'd just taken, much to Zak's satisfaction.

'25,000?!'

Well, actually it was 23,039 when I woke up this morning with 103 comments and 26,741 when I left the house to come here, then 29,328 when I sneaked a look on the way back from the park, Zak wanted to say. Only, he felt that Chloe might make another jibe about how pointless the video was and then say he was obsessed. He was getting that way, sure, but he didn't want her to know that.

'That's pretty impressive,' Chloe admitted. 'Still, it'll never beat proper football.'

'Hey up, Zak.' Mr Smith poked his head around the door, his face as jovial as ever. There was nothing like reading a Sunday newspaper from front to back with his feet up in front of the fire and one of his wife's blueberry muffins at his side to put him into a good mood. 'Thought I could hear the sound of Chloe losing on the Xbox.'

'Just look at the screen, Dad,' Chloe replied. 'I'm winning, okay?'

'That's nice, dear. Hey, Zak. Did I hear that right? You've got 25,000 views on your video?'

'You did,' he replied. 'Me and Dad uploaded it two days ago and yesterday morning it went crazy. It turns out that people love it.'

'Well you stick at it. You've got a talent there. You might as well make the most of it.'

'Thanks, Mr Smith.'

'There's one thing he doesn't have any talent at though,' Chloe chimed in, before pressing down her white controller's B button. Zak looked up only to see the back of his virtual net rippling once more. 'Too easy,' Chloe laughed. 'Too easy. I don't even need to score sweaty goals against you.'

YouTube subscribers: 1,023
Instagram followers: 801
Twitter followers: 245

'Hold on, not so fast.'

Zak's dad sprang up from the kitchen table, specks of milk flying across the room as his spoon became upended from the movement.

'But I have to go fast, I'm late,' Zak complained. Of course he was late. It was Monday, the worst of all the days, and he had school. 'I need to go and knock for Chloe in a second.'

'It'll only take a second. Look.' He gestured over toward the unmistakeable red header of *The Redwood Review*, the town's only newspaper (since 1884, it proudly proclaimed), lying crumpled on the kitchen table.

'Betty Crocker wins bowls raffle?' Zak read out the headline on the back cover.

'No, not that! Look inside. One page from the back. I had a little word with that reporter who was at the game yesterday. Think it might have done the trick.' He tapped his nose and winked.

Chloe wouldn't mind waiting for a minute or two – especially not after the grief she'd given him over his video. And he could just work his charm on Mr Ahmed, his form tutor, if he was late for registration. Zak flicked the back page over and was met with a picture of his team in celebration.

REDWOOD GO MARCHING ON

Promising youngsters qualify for the next round of the cup,
by Cynthia Johnson

The supremely talented Redwood Rovers u13s side booked their place in the last 16 of the county cup after an impressive 2-0 victory over Barton Town FC. Goals from Marcus Court and Chloe Smith sealed the victory, although a classy second half display from young maestro Zak Oxden proved to be the difference, the striker grabbing wonderful assists for both goals.

A constant menace throughout the second half, Oxden's floating delivery was headed home in the 55th minute by defender Court, who appeared to be nursing a nasty knee injury. Down by a goal, Barton threw caution to the wind but left themselves exposed at the back. A sharp burst of pace from Oxden saw him beat a defender and drive into the penalty area before squaring for Smith to tap in on 83 minutes.

'We've got some fantastic players coming through,' head coach and club secretary Adam Jones said. 'There's real talent. I've got

high hopes for players like Zak Oxden and Chloe Smith. All of my
players understand the importance of hard work and discipline.
We hope we can go further this year than last year, where we
reached the semi-final.'

If they are to do just that, it is evident that they will be relying
on the mercurial talent of Oxden and the goals of Smith.

Zak's eyes grew wider with every new paragraph. A classy
display. Constant menace. Mercurial talent. They were talking
about him! He imagined the thousands of houses in Redwood,
all waking up to eat their cornflakes and read their morning
newspapers and turning straight to page seventy-six to read
about him. 'Wow.' That seemed to be the only explanation he
could give. 'Do you think they really mean it?'

'Of course they do, son. You were top drawer yesterday.' He
ruffled Zak's hair. 'And what's even better is that I know you've
got more in you.'

'I know. I feel like I can play much better than I did yesterday,'
Zak agreed. 'I was hopeless in the first half. I couldn't stop
thinking about my videos.'

'You'll learn to cope with that. It was your first experience
of getting lots of views. The unusual will soon become normal.
Just so long as you keep on going like you are.'

'I will. Right, I've got to—'

'But what it seems,' his dad waved the newspaper at him, as
if to stop him leaving the house, 'is that people like what they
see. If the newspaper raves about your skills, do you know what
that means?'

Zak glanced another look at the clock next to the kitchen

doorframe. 08:27. He could feel his phone vibrating in his pocket. He was already two minutes late to Chloe's house. 'What, Dad?'

'It means that more people will rave about them. So, here's what I'm thinking.'

'Dad, I'm going to be seriously late for school.'

'Just a minute, son. You've got plenty of time to get to school. If people like watching your skills in a game, why don't we show them? Next game, I'll film your skills and we can edit them into a highlights package. Remember that roulette turn you did around the defender? That would look blooming brilliant on a video.'

It would. Zak had to admit that his dad was on to something. 'Sounds good. Right, see you, Dad.'

'Everyone loves seeing you do that skill.' When his dad got excited like this, there was no stopping him. Part of Zak was pleased that he had something to interest him, to distract him on the days where there was no work for him to go to. But the other part of Zak was getting increasingly nervous about getting to school on time.

'Yep, see you then.' He opened the door.

'And let's get something out tonight.'

'Deal,' Zak closed the door and sprinted to the back yard to get his bike, fumbling to get his phone out of his pocket.

Zak: Runnin late. C u at school?

Chloe: No surprise. C u then.

It wasn't until breaktime that Zak managed to see Chloe. After breathlessly apologising to Mr Ahmed and charming his way out of a note in his planner, Zak settled down into the corner of the classroom for his first lesson of the day, Geography. As Mr Hill babbled on about migration and push and pull factors, Zak found his mind wandering. Which skills routine could he try in his next video?

The corridors at breaktime were hustling and bustling as always. Pupils embraced their short allowances of freedom, spilling out onto the concrete of the playground and gathering in their random groups. For Zak, the corridors were even crazier than normal. Word about his video had spread quickly. People he didn't even know could be found watching it in the hallways, sneaking looks discreetly at the phones which they weren't supposed to have in their possession in school hours. 'Sick video,' a particularly bulky boy with flowing brown hair said to Zak. 'Yo, tag me in your next video, I beg you,' another called out. What should have been a two-minute walk to the playground took ten minutes by the time he'd been stopped and fist-bumped and hugged and congratulated. Two people he didn't know even asked for selfies with him. Madness. That was all Zak could think as he did his best to move through the sea of bodies. He'd never felt more aware of the eyes on him, the people that parted the way for him out of respect. Should he start walking around the school with his chest puffed out, loud and proud? He didn't know. He moved with the pressure of those eyes, feeling the weight of every step. It felt strange, to be watched so closely. Not like on the internet, where the eyes were on him but not really on him. This was real life, real attention and he didn't know what to do. He was exactly the same as he had been before the weekend, the last time he was in school. But to the other pupils, he couldn't have been more different. No longer was he Zak. He was TekkerZak.

Chloe, Chris, Josh and Marcus were almost finished by the time he got out to join them. They'd been playing a game of heads and volleys, one of Zak's favourites. He cursed himself, not because of missing the chance to play along with them, but because he'd marked out the time to go over the routine he'd dreamed up in his Geography lesson. Like all of the routines, he'd need to practise it. He found that he'd always drop the ball, fall over, miskick it, get his feet tangled, at first. The perfection that came on camera only came from hours and hours of training.

But he didn't have hours.

'Are you ever going to be on time?' Chloe asked sarcastically, rolling her eyes. 'We're just finishing off.' Zak breathlessly explained his lateness and apologised to Chloe before telling his friends about his new school status. Chloe nodded and said she was happy for him without ever appearing to be too genuine. Chris, on the other hand, became increasingly agitated. 'Ridiculous,' he exclaimed before appointing himself as Head of Security for Zak. It'd be his job, he announced, to make sure that nobody bothered Zak as he walked around the school. The others were all happy with the arrangement because it didn't affect them.

By the end of lunchtime, Zak was on the lookout for a new Head of Security. It would have been more useful employing a garden gnome than Chris.

12

YouTube subscribers: 1,233
Instagram followers: 1,016
Twitter followers: 441

Dropped again. Zak span one way, the ball the other. Desperately, he lunged but it was already too late. The ball had bounced and he'd have to start over again. Sure, it was a tough skill and a tough routine that he'd dreamed up that morning in Geography. Sure, he'd barely had time to practise it in break or lunch. But under the pressure of the camera, his brain couldn't consider those factors. Instead, all he felt was frustration.

'Aaarrrghhhh!'

'No worries, son,' came the calm voice from behind the camera. 'We'll go again. We've got ages until the sun goes down. Plenty of time for filming.'

Zak retrieved the ball and returned to his marker, breathing deeply to focus. Anything to shake those past failures from his mind. It still felt weird having the camera on him, as if every single movement he made was being performed under a microscope. He was putting himself on show to the world and had to make everything perfect. If there was even the slightest of flaws, what would his followers think of him?

But did perfect exist?

'Three . . . two . . . one . . . Go!' His dad raised a hand and then slashed it down through the air to indicate the camera was rolling. On cue, he took four steps forward until he knew his face was filling the camera. 'Yes, yes guys,' he heard himself saying, the energy and charisma bouncing off his surroundings. He didn't even have to think before he spoke anymore. He'd already said the words so many times that they flowed from his mouth with ease – even with the pressure of the camera. 'And I'm back for more. I've been working on some new moves and I can't wait to show you. No spoilers, though, you'll have to watch until the end.' He winked at the camera knowingly. 'All right, let's go!'

He jerked his body back to the mark. Forget the camera, he told himself over and over. Act natural. Like you're just down the park. He started off with some ground moves, manipulating the ball constantly from one foot to the other with the Socrates movement, rolling it backwards before knocking it across with the instep. Ten times, then he rolled it backwards and followed the ball's motion, performing stepovers backwards. Only, he'd found a way to make those early moves extra hard. He did so with his headband over his eyes – blindfolded! It was the perfect clickbait, the kind of move that viewers would watch and exclaim 'no way!' and then want to share with their friends and families. Stopping short of the camera, he raised his headband up to its natural position and winked once more. It felt so weird. To be interacting with a blank lens. No, act natural. You're just down the park. There's no camera, he told himself. The ball was stationary now, his marker two paces behind him. He rolled his foot back over the ball and then stopped it in one motion by moving his knee parallel to the floor. Pushing all of his weight back, he added all of the force he could muster on top of the ball and then released it with his knee. The ball sprung up, his ever obedient servant and he pushed it higher with his knee, then caught it between his two arms raised in a diamond above his head. Just like he'd practised and failed the previous day.

This was it: the finishing move. He spun round and round, the ball moving up and down and round and round his two arms, back and forth from his neck to his hands. He span out and this time the ball arced exactly where he wanted it. Quickly, he dropped to the floor in a press-up position and the ball nestled in the small dent of his back. Gratefully, Zak felt its leather hugging the outside of his t-shirt and knew that it was stationary. He dipped his triceps and manoeuvred his body to the ground to complete the press-up, then went back up with the ball still in the same place. Yes, that'd look good. He lifted his head, as if searching for the camera and as the ball moved down his back, he snapped his back heels forward. The connection was perfect. The ball flew from his right heel and catapulted into the goal. Casually, as if he hadn't already failed at that exact skill twenty times that same afternoon, he got to his feet and strolled up to the camera, moving as if inside he wasn't exploding with happiness. 'Tekkers,' he winked.

'And we're done.'

Now the rush was no longer locked inside his body but was joyfully escaping, all of the stress from his failures forgotten in an instant.

'That was sick, I know it was,' Zak shouted as he charged around the back yard. Every inch of his body was buzzing with the sense of achievement. He had to get this uploaded straight away. It would blow up once more. For sure.

'You did great, son. Your followers are going to love it. Come on, let's get it up. I don't even think it'll need an edit. Well, apart from the music and the explosions, of course.'

'Amazing.' He followed his dad into the house, leaving the ball safely in the back yard. Inside the laptop was already open, the browser already showing the red and white homepage of YouTube. In just a matter of minutes the video file had been uploaded to the computer and opened in iMovie for editing. The pair watched the footage – no longer than five minutes old – together. It was just as surreal as always. Zak watching Zak, analysing every single one of the moves that he'd only just been doing. His dad was right, they only needed to add the explosions and music, which took them five minutes.

'This one is going to be massive,' his dad whispered. '42,000 views to beat, right?' Every time Zak heard that number his heart fluttered. He couldn't believe that something he'd done, that he'd trained for, had become so big. It seemed ridiculous, preposterous, outrageous. But it had happened, and it was continuing to grow.

'That's right,' he whispered.

The sound of the door made them both jump. There was someone outside and once more Zak cursed himself. He'd been so caught up in filming that he'd forgotten Chloe was coming around to practise. Which was ridiculous, because every Monday at 7, once she'd done her homework and eaten her tea, Chloe would come around to practise. He glanced over to the clock and sure enough, the time was exactly 7pm.

She walked straight in as always when Zak opened the door. 'What's going on?' she asked. 'You ready?'

'We're just finishing off a video, won't be a minute.'

'Let's see it then.' Zak led her over to the laptop where his dad was working. She perched next to him, her white Nike Mercurial Superfly trainers looking pristine against the dull grey carpet.

'How are you doing, Chloe?' his dad asked. 'Great performance the other day.'

'Thanks, Dean.' Unlike Zak, Chloe felt comfortable calling her friends' parents by their first names. 'Another round down. I really hope we win the cup this year.'

'Don't we all. You were so unlucky to go out last year. But anyway, you want to watch this, right?' Chloe nodded her head solemnly. 'Okay, I'll leave you two to it, anyway. Zak, get it uploaded after if you're happy. I think it's good to go.' He pressed play and once more the on-screen Zak leapt into life. Chloe nodded along throughout. Zak took pride at her reaction to the blindfolded skills. There was even an audible gasp at the spinning diamond.

'What do you think, then?' he asked as the screen faded to black with a smattering of white writing encouraging viewers to like, comment, share and subscribe to @therealTekkerZak.

'Yeah, it's good. The video is good.'

'So you see it's not a waste of time?' he said triumphantly. He wanted to make the most of her compliment. If only he could prove her wrong, just like he'd proved that lanky defender wrong.

'Well, I wouldn't say it's a waste of time. It's good but just don't get carried away with it.'

'What about the 10,000 hours?' he shot back. He had her there. She'd said it herself. 10,000 hours to become an expert. And from her face, he could tell that she knew. She sighed, her eyes still on the screen.

'Look, this is all new. A few days ago you didn't want to be a freestyler. Your whole life had been about football, just like mine has been. Don't forget that, that's all I'm saying. Don't forget about football and your friends for some new craze that may only last a week.'

'It'll last longer than that,' he laughed.

'It might and I hope for your sake it does. Just think about it.' He didn't want to think about it. He wanted to get the video uploaded and to experience the rush once more. The thrill of adulation from people all around the world, people who didn't know him but soon would. 'Anyway, you ready?'

'I'll just get this uploaded. It won't take a minute. Well, maybe a bit longer because of my rubbish WiFi connection,' he joked.

'Fine. I'll be in the back yard.'

The door slammed shut and immediately the sound of the ball pounded the wall. He could picture his best mate now, working on her control with both feet by playing the ball against the back of his house with one touch, never letting it touch the floor, never letting it break any of the windows – just like Zak had done a few weeks before.

Following one final check, he clicked on the upload button in the top right hand corner of the screen. The bar flashed into life, displaying the grey loading bar. There was no stopping it now. The video was about to be released into the wild. He went to the sink and poured himself a glass of water as he waited. From this angle he could see Chloe working. She was totally focused on the ball, her ponytail swishing up and down with every step. She didn't notice Zak watching her. She never did when she was in the zone.

50% loaded. Why did they have to have such slow WiFi? Distractedly, he rolled his ball from foot to foot beneath the table, impatient at the internet speed. Pound. Pound. Pound. Chloe was into her rhythm. He let the noise take him away, willing the video to upload so he could join her. Yes, done. The screen flashed and there it was, the video live and public.

The pounding stopped and the back door swung open. 'Are you ever coming?' He could tell she was getting irritated now.

'Yes, sure. I've just got to put it on Instagram too and then I'll be there.'

'Fine.' Her voice was thick with undisguised boredom, her full-stops the loudest words she spoke. 'Put it on Instagram and then come out here. It's fun to pass to a wall but more fun to pass to an actual human being.'

'Yeah, yeah,' he replied absent-mindedly. In truth, he'd barely heard the end of her sentence. He was too focused on the video. He'd already had the first like from someone on YouTube and he was sure there were more to come.

Chloe sighed. She'd known Zak since they were tiny. They'd grown up together, taken their first steps together, been best mates for as long as they could both remember. They knew everything about each other, and Chloe knew that right then his thoughts were miles away.

'Hurry up. I'll see you out there,' she said, slamming the door once more.

'Cool,' muttered Zak in reply, his bright blue eyes still glued to the screen. Instagram. He unlocked his phone and uploaded the shortened version of the video that his dad had edited to his page, asking his followers to watch the full version on his YouTube. Right, done. Although, he'd best check on the YouTube views again. It'd only take a second or two.

Thirty views. Two comments. It had only been live for a couple of minutes. And now the notifications were coming through on his phone. His insides jumped. This was the thrill, the rush. Refresh, refresh, refresh, all the while seeing more views. The numbers weren't massive but they were more. Right now more was important. Another new subscriber. Another comment. People knew a good video when they saw it.

'I'm going home now.' Chloe had opened the back door again. 'See you at school tomorrow.'

'But I'm just coming now.' Zak started, then stopped just as quickly. When did it get dark outside? He checked his phone. 21:15. Disbelievingly, he checked his laptop screen, then the clock on the wall. They were all in agreement. 21:15. Where had the time gone? He'd let his best mate down. He'd have to make it up to her, that was for sure. He'd go around her house the next evening, put in an extra intense session. He'd – wait

– the flashing notifications on his phone distracted him. Now he reached for the screen and pulled up and down to refresh the screen.

One new follow.

@aboutrabt

That was when Zak truly went crazy.

YouTube subscribers: 1,676
Instagram followers: 1,189
Twitter followers: 526

Friday was the easiest day to wake up on. Knowing that it was the last day of the school week, kicking off with PE, made the sky seem a little bluer, the clouds a little less grey. And most importantly, it was the day before Saturday: Zak's favourite day of the week. He knew he wasn't the only Redwood Rovers player who felt the same way.

Yet no matter how early he got up, his dad would be sitting at the kitchen table with a bowl of cornflakes and a cup of English breakfast tea with the newspaper open. 'Orange juice?' he offered Zak, who nodded. He got a bowl from the cupboard and poured it full of muesli, which Mr Jones advised due to its excellent source of slow release carbohydrates. He probably didn't advise the extra sugar and dried fruit Zak put on top of the cereal, but Zak had no intention of telling him that much.

'Got something else for you,' he smiled. 'I didn't just speak to that reporter about the game, you know.' *The Redwood Review* was open in front of him. Friday was its special sports preview of the weekend, looking ahead to all of the weekend's fixtures. But the article that shouted out at Zak from the table wasn't a preview of Redwood's league game against Littleton. It had nothing to do with Redwood Rovers. But it had everything to do with Zak.

SOCCER SUPERSTAR'S PLEA
By Cynthia Johnson

Talented footballer Zak Oxden is taking his game to the next level. The youngster from King's Lane, Redwood, is already regarded as one of the best players in the area. Now, he's taking his skills to the world. His YouTube videos of his football flicks and tricks has gone viral, earning rave reviews from places as far as Brazil and China. As of Wednesday evening, his most watched video had received 39,816 views.

'We always knew Zak's football skills were special,' his father, Dean Oxden said. 'We wanted to share them with the world – and the world likes them.'

Zak plans to step up his content output and create his own series of videos to inspire and entertain fans around the globe. He's looking for support from Redwood to make this possible.

'I'm trying to do the best I can for Zak,' said Dean. 'But to really take the next step we're looking for sponsors. That will help us to source better equipment, allowing the videos to be filmed in better

quality and edited with the latest software. With your support, we can produce top notch videos which will be seen around the world.

'Our last video had nearly 40,000 views. That's 40,000 people who could be seeing your business.'

To support Zak on his journey, please email Dean Oxden on dean0@messenger.com. Follow Zak's videos on @therealTekkerZak

Zak read the article once. Then twice. Then three times. The feeling didn't change.

'We need this, son,' the familiar voice said from the next chair over, attempting to be as reassuring as possible. 'I don't know how long it'll take to get any money from YouTube. I don't even know if we've got any money from YouTube yet, have we?' Zak didn't have a clue. 'But if someone helps us out with a bit of money, we help them out with a bit of a promotion. It's like a football team having a shirt sponsor.'

'No, it's cool,' Zak replied with a smile. He had realised something very important. As he read the newspaper, he realised that he was becoming used to being seen. He'd noticed it in the school corridors, where the eyes that followed him were now normal. Watching himself on phones and laptops and tablets was now normal, no longer so surreal. The unusual had become normal. This was just another incident. 'It's great, in fact. If someone wants to pay us then that's perfect.'

'You know it makes sense.' His dad put his arm around him and ruffled his hair.

'Get off!' he complained, trying to escape his dad's grip.

'And look at this.' His dad produced a box from underneath the table. CANON Powershot G7 X MKII: Compact Camera

Vlogging Kit, read the black letters. 'It's got a 1:1.8-2.8 zoom lens and 20 megapixels,' he explained. 'Plus a wireless connection so we can put it straight on the laptop. It also comes with a tripod. It'll be so much easier to shoot with a steady hand.'

'Can I take a look?' Zak asked, already reaching for the camera from its box. It was sleek and black, a beautiful design. He turned it over in his hand. So this was the tool that'd turn him into a star.

'We'll give it a little run out tonight. Nothing big, we don't want you tired for the game. There's no work for me today so I'll make sure it's all in order and I know how to use the film setting.'

'Make sure you click record this time.' His dad chuckled at that. He didn't mind laughing at himself. 'I can't wait for the game tomorrow.'

'Nor can I.'

The game would have extra meaning with his dad's camera rolling from the sideline. It was only a league game – and Redwood were comfortably winning their league, nine points ahead of their closest challengers – but now there'd be extra eyes on Zak in every game. People knew who he was. His followers wanted him to do well. And Cynthia Johnson was hungry for stories.

Zak knew that if he performed well in the next day's game it could only help his chances of being sponsored. Cynthia Johnson would be more likely to write another article. His videos would get more views, and who knew who would be watching? There would perhaps be an agent on the sidelines, or even a scout from the local professional club, High Grove FC. The possibilities made Zak fizz with anticipation.

He was ready. He'd enjoyed two good training sessions with Redwood Rovers that week. He'd done his best to patch things up with Chloe, putting in the hours together as the pair worked hard to improve their shooting and first touch. They'd devised a routine where Chloe passed the ball powerfully into Zak, who had to control it and set the ball for Chloe to hammer into the empty net. Once that was done they went again. And again. And again. Until each had improved. Already Zak was looking forward to practising with her again after school. To add the final touches needed to shine the next day.

Yes, tomorrow was going to be a good day.

14

YouTube subscribers: 2,026
Instagram followers: 1,320
Twitter followers: 616

This was the arena. His arena. As Zak glided around Redwood's pitch he felt close to perfection. Everything was right. The team were winning 3-0. His skills were coming off. He was controlling everything. He'd already scored twice, a delicate chip from eighteen yards and a tap-in at the back post. Chloe bagged the other, her finish from the edge of the penalty area from his set back an exact replica of what they'd been training all week. And the camera on the side was capturing everything. It was going to make for an amazing video.

'Keep going, Zak,' his father encouraged from the sideline. 'This is golden.' Zak gave him a thumbs-up and then immediately went in pursuit of the ball. He loved the games where it felt like he could do no wrong. Confidence flowed from his golden boots. A Littleton defender raced in and he rolled the ball through their legs to nutmeg them. The crowd roared in appreciation, then roared again when Zak slowed, allowing the defender to catch up with him again, then rolled the ball back exactly where it came from, nutmegging the defender once more.

Could he do no wrong?

The more he created, the tighter Littleton's defenders got to him. They wouldn't let him take a step without tracking his movement. Zak dropped a stepover to beat one, a roulette to beat two, jinked his way past a third and played a pass out to the wing. Still, the wall of opponents came back, and now they were getting angry. Nobody made fools out of them. But the angrier they got, the rasher their challenges, the easier Zak could beat them. He sensed two pairs of studs flying toward his shins and bunny hopped up with the ball between his feet. The studs missed, aimed too low, and the player slid underneath him. 'Woah,' he heard someone from the crowd scream, then 'watch out Zak!' There was another player charging at him. He let the ball drop to the ground so it bounced on the turf, then carefully flicked it up in the air and jumped once more. The player went sliding past man and ball. 'You've sent him to the hot dog stand!' Chris laughed.

And he wasn't done there.

Zak dropped deep to collect a pass from Josh, then swerved past his opponent like she wasn't even there. Then he was off, charging at the back-pedalling defence. He drove at the heart of the defence, right in the centre. He could see that they were panicking. They didn't know whether to move forward and block his path or keep on dropping back. The captain, a wiry ferret of a player, charged. He faked to his left, before neatly hooking a toe around the ball and jinking in the opposite direction, leaving the captain stranded as he darted free. Another defender, this time the other centre back. She was running in way too fast. Greedily, Zak licked his lips at the open space behind her. The full backs wouldn't be able to catch him. He slowed a little, drawing the defender in with his deft touches. Then, when she was within two paces of him, he trapped the ball between the heel of his front foot and instep of his back foot. With the back foot he rolled it up, then flicked it over his and the defender's head. She hadn't expected that. A rainbow flick, a sombrero, a Lambretta, whatever his followers called that skill, Zak knew they'd love seeing that. He caught the ball on the second bounce and raced forward once more, breaking into the penalty area.

'Square it! Square it!'

The goalkeeper had sensed what was going to happen early on and had already raced off her line, moving to narrow his shooting angle. It was too late to chip her. There was only a small area of the net left open. The easy option was to pass it across the area for Chloe. She had a tap-in. It was a certain goal.

But there was just one thought going through Zak's head. His dad's video camera.

He knew this could go viral. It'd be picked up by all the national papers, the football showboat accounts, it'd be seen by hundreds of thousands, maybe even millions. All he had to do was finish it off.

Zak squared the keeper up. He'd done this hundreds of times before. He drew his foot back, then shifted its position just before contact. Rather than shoot, rather than pass, he moved the ball to his right in a flash of gold. The keeper would expect the shot, not the dribble.

Only she didn't.

As Zak attempted to dribble around the keeper, she made a desperate lunge through the air and smothered the ball, collecting Zak as she went and sending him tumbling head over heels.

'Penalty!' he screamed out of desperation. The referee waved play on.

'Well done, goalkeeper,' the referee said. 'That's a fair challenge.'

Zak lay flat out in the penalty area, staring up at the sky. Slowly he turned his head to see Chloe, still standing in exactly the same position. She was staring at him, confused, totally stationary.

'Why didn't you square it? I was open.'

Zak didn't know what to say. He got to his feet, brushed himself down and looked meekly toward Chloe.

'Sorry.' That was all he could say. 'Sorry.'

Mr Jones grimaced on the sideline, his hands on his hips. Cynthia Johnson furiously scribbled notes. Even Zak's dad temporarily stopped filming. Chloe glared at him, hands on hips, and then she was gone, back in the game, running about to make something happen.

Yet as Zak returned to the game he realised that he wasn't sorry that he didn't pass the ball to Chloe. He was sorry that the keeper had stopped him from scoring.

It was a relief when the final whistle blew. The mistake hadn't cost the team. They'd won 3-0. Zak had put in a great performance and they'd have some great content. His dad ran onto the pitch with the camera to get close-up shots of the end of game handshakes. He said his 'well dones' and 'good games' and made the most of his display of sportsmanship. With the camera no longer recording, he turned to look for Chloe.

She was gone.

There was no sign of her. He jogged back to the changing room, past the parents returning to their cars, empty coffee mugs in hand. Past the brothers and sisters who had joined in support. Past the players, some of them already stripped of their boots, socks and shinpads. She was in the small changing room, putting on her tracksuit bottoms and fresh Adidas Stan Smith trainers. She didn't look up as Zak entered. 'Sorry about that,' he repeated and now she looked. 'I should have squared it.'

'You should have done a lot,' she shot back.

'What do you mean?' Zak had done a lot. He'd torn through his opponents like they weren't there, had scored two, assisted another. He deserved a break – especially from his best mate. Come to think of it, she'd been acting funny for the whole week.

'You need to separate the two. Your freestyling is cool but it's not football. You can't just go onto a pitch and do all of your skills instead of playing properly. What about those two nutmegs? They looked great, but you won't be able to do them against a better team. You won't be able to do them in the county cup final. You should have passed the ball to me then. I was in acres of space and could have got a shot off. But no, you wanted to impress the camera.'

'Look, I said I'm sorry I didn't pass,' Zak protested.

'It wasn't just about the pass,' she said as she got to her feet and stormed through the door, her final parting shot.

Zak put his head in his hands and stared at the floor, breathing deeply so that he could think straight. Chloe would calm down, he was sure of it. And now he was thinking straight, he realised that nothing had changed. The only thing that he regretted was not scoring his hat-trick.

YouTube subscribers: 2,631
Instagram followers: 1,591
Twitter followers: 723

It didn't take long for the email to arrive. Within forty-eight hours of the newspaper article, his dad's inbox lit up with a message from Brown's Sporting Goods. And not just any message. It wasn't because he needed a racket restringing or a pair of cycling shorts. It was because they had an offer for Zak.

Excitedly, his dad printed off the email and stuck it to the fridge. 'We're on our way,' he beamed. Zak could only agree.

Dear Mr Oxden,

I read your son's newspaper article with interest. My name is Darren Brown, owner of Brown's Sporting Goods on Redwood High Street. You might have been in my shop before.

There is no doubt that your son has a special talent. I want to grow my business and collaborating with Zak makes perfect sense.

This Friday I'm receiving a big stock order of new boots. I want to make sure I have plenty of customers. What do you say to your son showing off some of his skills in my shop that evening? I'll make sure it's worth his while. How about a £100 voucher to use in my shop?

Yours,

Darren Brown

A £100 voucher! Think of what he could get with that. Another pair of golden Panther Sport boots. Or maybe the latest Nike Phantom VSN boots, the ones with the refined kangaroo leather that provided cushioned control and explosive power. And what about a pair of training trousers, the ones that tapered around the legs like Chloe had? He could get a few cones, use them to dribble around and mark out spaces rather than having to rely on jumpers and whatever objects he could find. Perhaps he could use the personalisation service to get his YouTube handle stitched onto his boots. The possibilities seemed endless.

'This is so sweet,' Zak replied. It really was. He'd always bought his kit from Brown's Sporting Goods. He went into the shop regularly with Chloe, looking up at all of the football boots on the wall and deciding his favourite. He usually found himself drawn to the brightest, flashiest boots, so long as they were made by one of the big brands like Nike, Adidas, Puma or Panther Sports.

'Yes, but £100? We're better than that, Zak. I'm going to tell him we'll only do it for £200.'

'£200?' Zak wasn't so sure. He didn't want to put the £100 at risk by asking for too much. It seemed dangerous. They were still getting used to this. It was all new to them. But then what else did his dad have? An unreliable work schedule, a table full of demands for bill payments and a distant reminder of the better times he'd previously experienced in his life. Zak thought of how his dad had embraced his new passion, the editing work he'd already done, how it left him more excited than he'd been in ages.

'Look, I can see you're not sure. You've got to be tough in this situation. This is business.' His dad tapped his nose knowingly, speaking in his most reassuring voice. 'I'll give him a call now.'

It was an agonising wait while his dad was on the phone. He said yes and no and contorted his face, but five minutes later the deal was done. Darren Brown promised to put up posters of Zak all around his shop and place an article in *The Redwood Review* to encourage people to come and see Zak's skills. He also promised to pay £200.

'Business,' his dad repeated, tapping his nose once more. 'And talking of business, we've got a new film to edit.'

'Would you mind doing it?' Zak asked. He'd planned a game of headers and volleys with Chloe, Josh, Marcus and Chris over at the park. Once again, he found himself needing to patch up his relationship with his best mate and as usual, football seemed the best way to do it.

'It'll be better with you. You know all of the moves. And I was thinking you could commentate as the skills play out on the video. I've got you a little microphone for it.' His dad showed him a little stand with a ball of wires. It did sound a good idea.

'Can't we do it later? I've got a kickabout with my mates.'

'It won't take long. If you go to that kickabout I know you'll be gone all day and then it'll be too late. I know it's a quick turnaround but that's what your followers want. The more we post – and the quicker we post it – the bigger your channel will become.'

What his dad said made perfect sense. Zak knew he should work on his video, but he also knew that his friends were relying on him. They were going to have a laugh together, to relax after the game the previous day and then have lunch and play *FIFA* round Chloe's. He didn't want to miss out on that. But he didn't want to miss out on the video. What if his dad was absolutely right and he missed out on loads of followers because the video was released too late? He'd been right about Darren Brown, after all. He'd never forgive himself if he lost out on followers. No, his friends wouldn't mind him being late for one kickabout. They'd had thousands of kickabouts over the years and they'd have thousands more after this one.

'How long do you reckon it will take?'

Zak's dad looked at his watch.

'Well, we've got 90 minutes of action. We'll probably put that into a 90-second highlights video. Shouldn't take more than three hours?'

'Three hours!' That ruled out the morning. But he still had all afternoon and evening for a kickabout and *FIFA*. His dad's face looked up at him from the laptop, excited, expectant, surrounded by all of the new gear that he hadn't known existed just two weeks before.

'Fine. But let's be quick.' Guilty at his soon-to-be absence, Zak unlocked his phone and opened WhatsApp to the group he had with his friends.

REDWOOD LEGENDS
ZAK: Bn delayed. Sry. Will miss the park and c u at Chloes? There @ 1
JOSH: Sorry 2 hear that
MARCUS: That sucks
CHRIS: No worries man
CHLOE: K

K

Typical Chloe. She just preferred her personality to shine through in person. That's what Zak told himself, though in reality he knew that she was still annoyed with him. The simple 'K' was a universal message of frustration. He'd have some serious patching up to do later on.

Zak tried to ignore his nagging doubts as he went through the match footage on screen. The new camera had worked wonders. The footage was clean and crisp and the zoom function made sure that Zak was always front and centre of the shot. His dad's steady hand, combined with Zak's silky control, made for some great content – even better than how Zak had remembered it happening. He sat open-mouthed at the ease he seemed to move the ball around the pitch, totally absorbed in the action. Together, they watched the entire 90-minute match in 2x speed, stopping the footage whenever Zak had the ball at his feet. 'How about this?' his dad suggested as Zak took out two defenders with a pass down the right wing.

'Stick it in the maybes,' he replied. 'I know I do better stuff in this game.' The pass was good, but it wasn't the kind of move to get a viewer up off their seat in disbelief. It was good for a football video, but not a freestyle video. Not enough 'wow' factor, Zak thought.

'Right you are.' The video played once more on fast forward.

'Look, stop it here. This is where I do the bunny hops,' Zak said, pointing at the screen. 'We've got to get this in. Look at that defender slide past me!'

'That's a definite.'

'Chris said I sent him to the hot dog stand. I'll definitely use that one in the commentary.'

They clipped the footage then sped on the match once more. Zak watched as his mates moved the ball around at lightning pace. Then suddenly he had the ball and they slowed it right down again. 'Okay, clip this whole bit. This is the rainbow flick section.'

There the defenders were – and then there they weren't, as the ball floated over them and Zak raced forward. Slowed down, he could see Chloe's movements even more clearly. She'd read exactly what was going to happen and knew where to move. How stupid he'd been to try and dribble around the keeper! From this angle he could see everything so much more clearly. He should have just slotted the ball through her legs. That would have looked even better. 'Can we make it so it looks like the keeper fouls me?'

'I'll do my best,' his dad replied. 'I'll zoom out so you can't see as clearly and then you can shout penalty in the commentary?'

'Deal.'

'Right, I think that's us then.'

The whole process had taken two hours of searching and discussing. The result was five minutes of content, from Zak walking on to the pitch to his two goals, his assists, his skills and his handshakes at the final whistle.

'I look like a baller in this!' exclaimed Zak.

'That's the plan,' his dad winked. 'But let's cut it down to 90 seconds. That way we only include the very best bits.'

After another 30 minutes they were done. The highlights video was ready to be uploaded. His two goals had made the cut, so had his bunny hop, nutmegs, rainbow flick, all mashed together to create pure tekkers. His dad passed him the microphone. 'Just be as excitable as always, I know your followers will love it.'

'Yes, yes guys,' Zak shouted into the microphone. 'This is Zak and today I'm going to be showing you some in-game tekkers . . . so here's my team: Redwood Rovers. Shout out to our coach Mr Jones and all of my teammates.' The video switched from the kick-off to Zak's first goal. 'So here's Chloe on the ball. She's some player. Destined for the top, mark my words. And she's passed it to me and oh my gosh, have you seen that, I've just chipped the keeper. I had no right, no right to do that. Can we get a replay on that?' Obligingly the REPLAY button that his dad had found on the internet flashed in the top left corner and the chip replayed. 'Ooohhh,' Zak added. 'Tekkers.' It wasn't in his nature to be so arrogant. Usually, he let his feet do the talking. From watching other YouTubers, though, he knew that he needed to play a part. Acting flashily and being super-confident was infectious. That was why he shouted out with so much energy. And the more that he did it, the more that he liked it.

Another twenty minutes. After five attempts, he finally nailed a version they were both happy with. He rushed to the sink and poured a glass of water. His throat felt so dry from all of that shouting.

'Right, I'll get this uploaded,' Zak's dad said. 'You can go and see Chloe.'

'Not yet,' Zak replied, his glass of water already drunk. 'I want to see how this performs.' His friends could wait. What was another half hour when he'd already delayed their kickabout by so much time?

Need bit longer, he messaged the group. *Only 15, promise.* He put his phone to the side, not bothering to wait for a response. All of his focus was on the screen.

The likes soon came in their hundreds.

YouTube subscribers: 2,656
Instagram followers: 1,601
Twitter followers: 801

The highlights reel had climbed to 7,104 views by the time Zak managed to peel himself away from the screen. It was on course to be his best performing video by far and no wonder. Many of his ever-growing army of subscribers received a notification every time he uploaded a video. They'd watch it, share it and then bring in more viewers, who'd repeat the process.

Zak pocketed his phone so he could continue to check the views and likes on his video and set off on the short walk to Chloe's. 1.45pm. He was only a little later than agreed.

Mrs Smith answered the door with a smile. 'Hello Zak! I've just been reading about you in my paper. Exciting, isn't it?'

'Yes, Mrs Smith,' Zak replied, his cheeks reddening.

'I'm pleased you're doing well. Come in, come in. I'll just find Chloe.'

Zak stepped into the welcoming house and made himself comfortable on the sofa, wishfully sniffing the chocolate cake that he could tell was being baked in the oven. Instinctively, he reached for his phone. 7,896 views. 583 likes. 75 comments – just three of them negative. Still, those three comments bit at Zak. He clicked onto their profiles and stared at their photos. Why did they not like the video? Were they just trolls, there to make others feel worse? Were they jealous? Or did they just think it was no good?

'She's in the garden.' Mrs Smith had returned from her search. 'Why don't you get your shoes back on and join her?'

Chloe's ponytail bounced up and down as she dribbled from left to right. Zak recognised what she was doing instantly. Ajax footwork: routines involving lots of quick touches on both feet using different parts of each foot. Laces. Sole. Inside. Out. It was one of her favourite practices. Mr Jones swore by it.

'There's no better way to develop your game than by touching the ball,' he enjoyed telling his players.

Chloe reached the end of her exercise, then started another without even looking at him.

'You not waiting for me then?' he asked. She ignored him, all of her focus on manipulating the ball with each foot.

Zak shrugged. He'd seen Chloe in every kind of mood over the years, both good and bad.

'Suit yourself,' he muttered, retrieving a ball from the corner of the garden and following Chloe as she dribbled. His presence made her go even faster. Zak struggled to keep up as Chloe darted around the cones. Every touch with her white Nikes was perfectly weighted, her confidence using both feet evident. After a couple of minutes, when she realised Zak wasn't going to stop following her, she came to a halt. Sweat dripped down her face, strands of her long blonde hair stuck to her forehead.

'What took you so long?'

Zak had been expecting the question. 'I had to help dad with something.'

'It wasn't another of those videos, was it?'

'No,' he lied.

'Are you sure? Because I saw your dad with a camera filming our game yesterday.' She folded her arms, raising one eyebrow at Zak in a look of total accusation.

He'd been rumbled. Quickly, Zak searched for an excuse.

'He filmed the game so I could analyse my performance. It's easier to see how I can improve when I watch it back on the screen.'

'So I won't see it on YouTube then?' she responded.

'Well we might make it into a video,' he spluttered. 'I mean, we played well. All of us. We look great.'

Chloe sighed. She flicked her ball up and caught it.

'It's cool what you're doing, Zak,' she said. 'But I've said it once and I'll say it again. Don't get carried away with it. I'm worried about you. You're acting differently. You wouldn't have done those unnecessary skills in the game before this all started. You would have squared that pass instead of going for glory. We're a team, remember? But recently it's been more like each of us out for ourselves. Like all you care about is showing off for your "fans".' She spat out that final word. Fans. It made him shudder.

'It's under control,' he assured her, wondering whether he'd broken the 10,000-view mark yet. 'We're still a team.'

'Good,' Chloe replied. 'Because I can train by myself. But it's always better to have someone with me. And we're much stronger as a team than apart.'

'You know that.' Zak offered his fist. Chloe eyed him, no longer accusatory but nor friendly. She left him hanging, trying to work it out. And then slowly, so slowly, she raised her hand and accepted the fist-bump. 'Hey, where are the others?' Zak asked. It had only just hit him that none of them were there.

Chloe rolled her eyes. At least the accusatory look was gone. 'Chris's dad saw him at the park and went mad. He was supposed to be grounded. Marcus needed to do homework and Josh wanted to watch the rest of some Netflix series.'

'What did you do to them?' Zak laughed. 'I thought you were only playing headers and volleys!'

'We did.'

'Oh well. Quick game of *FIFA*? I owe you a beating from the other day.'

'You've got no chance,' Chloe laughed. A sign of friendship. He'd broken through the steely exterior, ducked past the accusatory look and reclaimed his best mate. He could always back himself to patch up the relationship. He just had to back himself much more regularly these days.

'You set up, I'll just nip to the toilet.'

Zak took his muddy trainers off at the back door to keep Mrs Smith happy and made for the bathroom. He locked the door, then reached straight into his pocket.

11,706 views.

109

Energy buzzed throughout his body. Quickly, he scrolled through the comments. A few more negative. But a lot more positive. Plenty more subscribers. He refreshed again.

How long had he been? Too long. Zak put his phone back into his pocket and flushed the toilet to cover his tracks and opened the door. Chloe would never suspect a thing.

YouTube subscribers: 2,944
Instagram followers: 1,756
Twitter followers: 859

Zak felt them before he saw them. One second he was walking through the school corridor. The next he'd been slammed against the wall. He cried in surprise as the full force cracked through his body, bashing his left shoulder against a display of work on equality and tolerance. 'Hello superstar,' one laughed. 'What are you doing over there?'

'He's not such a big man now, is he?' another voice said.

By the time Zak had collected his bearings they were gone. What had he done? He flashed around confused, desperately trying to see who had done it. But it was hopeless. The pockets of pupils had closed in once more. All he could see was a blur of green blazers. Why would they do that on purpose? He'd never done anything to upset anybody.

Cautiously, he dusted himself off and carried on into the playground. It was lunchtime. Kickabout time. He'd just forget it ever happened.

By now he was well known in school. To some he was the internet famous kid. To many he was @therealTekkerZak. No longer did he feel awkward having people watching him walk around school. He didn't give it a second thought. In fact, he embraced it. The unusual had become the normal. The attention became enjoyable. Never quite as enjoyable as the ecstatic comments he received from around the world, but still enjoyable. It was nice to be known. So when people stared at him he smiled back and said hello. He didn't worry about the eyes on him. Nor did he worry about the nudges and whispers.

Not until the incident.

On Thursday they targeted him again. This time Zak saw their faces. Three of them, big enough to be year 11s. 'Hey superstar, sick videos,' said the ringleader, a hulking figure with a skinhead and a scowl. Disgust dripped through his words. It was clear he didn't think Zak's videos were sick. Worst of all, Zak recognised the voice. It was the same one that had sounded before he was slammed into the wall. He scanned his surroundings. For a school of over 1,000 pupils there was practically nobody about. Just a couple of stragglers rushing to their final lesson of the day. If only he hadn't taken his time to get to science. If only he hadn't gone to the bathroom and had walked with Josh. Right now, he'd much rather be sitting through Mrs Sprockett's presentation on electrons. He'd rather be anywhere than here.

'He thinks he's too important for the school, doesn't he?'

another opened his mouth. He was wearing a hoodie – enough to give Mrs Turnbull a heart attack. A packet of cigarettes poked out of his pocket.

'Someone needs to bring him back to earth,' the third suggested, advancing menacingly.

Zak was in danger, that much was clear. He had mere seconds to make a decision. Fight or flight. He had no chance. There was one of him and three of them. And they were all massive. No, he wouldn't stand a chance. He could shout for help, but what if nobody heard him? Zak's blood ran cold. His heart boomed out of his chest, every beat quicker than the one before. They were five paces from him. Soon they'd be on top of him in a whirr of fists and feet and punches and kicks. He couldn't bear to picture it. There was only one option.

Zak ran. He ran and ran and didn't care what happened as long as he wasn't caught. It was a calculated move. Speed was one of his main assets and with the walkways so quiet he'd have a clear run at the science department. 'After him!' came the cry from the group's leader. He could hear footsteps pounding the paving behind him. He ran with all of his energy, pushing away from the ground and pumping his arms as if his life depended on it. Which, in a way, it did. All along the length of the school building he ran. Surely, someone would see him. Why weren't they stopping those chasing him? The path followed the building round and Zak ran with it. There it was: the science building. He was twenty yards away. He stole a glance over his shoulder. They'd underestimated his pace. The leader's face was puffy, the effort proving tough for him. Ten yards. He was going to make it.

'Oxden!' Mr Davies, the assistant headteacher stood in the doorway to the science department, his cheeks red with anger. 'What on earth do you think you're doing? You know you're not allowed to run in this school.'

'I . . . I was being chased, sir,' Zak explained breathlessly. 'I was being threatened.'

'I don't see anybody.' Mr Davies's voice was still raised. 'Where are you supposed to be?'

'Mrs Sprockett's, sir. I've got science.'

'Fine, *walk* there and then once the bell rings I want you to walk to my office. You can explain yourself there.'

'You mean detention?'

'You'll find out what I mean.' Mr Davies turned on his heel, his face still bright red. If ever there was a man who enjoyed being angry it was him. Detention, Zak reflected, was the best that he could hope for with Mr Davies. Still, it was much better than what could have happened. He was safe. For now.

Mr Davies, it turned out, was a man of his word. First, Zak endured another painful science lesson where time seemed to stand still. Mrs Sprockett gave him a grilling for being late and put his name instantly on the board for bad behaviour, then droned on about chemical reactions. He focused as best he could, doing everything to not get another warning, which would see him being sent out of the class. Finally, finally the bell rang and allowed Zak to escape from one prison to another: Mr Davies's room.

Right in the heart of the school, down a corridor that few pupils ever stepped in, lay Mr Davies's room. Right next to the headmistress Mrs Cooper's office, it proudly proclaimed his name on a bland sign. The door was always shut. Zak knocked two times and Mr Davies's voice barked back. 'Come in.' The room was just as bland as he had expected. The walls were white, a single bookcase of neatly labelled folders and a framed degree certificate the only decoration in the room. Mr Davies sat upright, his eyes fixed intensely on Zak. He gestured to the chair on the other side of his grand mahogany desk and Zak sat.

'One: why were you late? Two: why were you running?' Zak gulped. He'd have to put on a performance to stop Mr Davies's face turning an even brighter shade of red.

'Sorry, sir. I went to the toilet between lessons, that's why I was late. And then this gang of boys saw me and threatened me.'

'What did they say?' Mr Davies leaned forward in his chair, fingers resting on his grey lips. At Redwood Community College, there was a saying that 'snitches get stitches'. Pupils were taught by the older pupils not to grass up on their fellow pupils. Nobody liked a grass. But being threatened wasn't much fun either.

'They said that I needed bringing back down to earth. That I think I'm too important for the school.'

'Mm hmm,' Mr Davies responded. Zak wondered whether he was enjoying this. 'Well, it seems you do think you're too important to obey the school's rules. Running. And are those trainers?' He motioned down at Zak's feet. Instinctively, he pushed his feet under the table.

'No, sir.'

'And who were they?'

'I don't know, sir. I've never noticed them before. They looked like year 11s. There was a skinhead, another who was smaller and wearing a black hoodie, then one with long brown hair down to his shoulders. Oh, and that one was wearing a hairband.'

'Hmm. Okay. Let a teacher know if they bother you again. For now, I want you to sit in my room and write me a short report on chemical reactions. You were ten minutes late to class so you have ten minutes to complete the work. Being late is an inconvenience to everyone,' he sneered. 'You must learn that.'

The only thing Zak had learned, he reflected, was to watch himself. Success, it seemed, came at a price.

18

YouTube subscribers: 3,834
Instagram followers: 1,902
Twitter followers: 981

All eyes were on him. In this moment he could send them to
their feet, let their cheers ring to the ceiling, entertain them
like never before. Zak kept it simple to start with. He had to.
This was the first time he'd performed in front of an audience
bigger than Chloe and his dad. There they stood, no more than
a few metres in front of him, breathing the same air as him,
smelling the same fresh smell of newly unboxed boots that he
was smelling. There were around twenty of them, a mix of ages
all looking on expectantly. It was nothing like doing it in front
of camera. When the camera was watching he could make
mistakes. He could drop the ball and start again. In front of a
crowd that simply wasn't an option. He couldn't edit out any
mistakes. Everything had to be perfect.

He hadn't felt this nervous in a long time.

A rainbow flick to start, just like he'd done in the game. When he'd uploaded the highlights video, so many of the comments had been in awe of the move. As he rolled the ball up to the top of his heel and then flicked it over his head he could feel the crowd approve. The weight of expectation went up a level, but his own relief helped to put him at ease. It was a simple execution and there were more complex moves to follow. He kept the ball up with his right foot, then arced the foot around the ball with each keepy-up: consecutive around the world movements. On camera he could now do them without even thinking. In front of a crowd, however, the pressure of the eyeballs weighed heavily. Each one of them followed the ball up and down, letting him know that if he messed up he was done. But now he was into his rhythm. It was time to ramp up his performance. He caught the ball on his neck, flicked it up, then caught it again. Dangerously, it didn't stick on his neck the second time but rolled a little to the right. Zak swooped with his body, following the ball's path and tilting his shoulder up to return it to the centre. Not fast enough. The ball bounced onto the floor and inside Zak crumbled. It was over! He'd ruined it. A failure. He motioned to scream, to curse himself, and then he remembered where he was. This wasn't his back yard. He wasn't just facing a camera. He was facing an expectant crowd who wanted to be entertained. There was still time to rescue the performance.

Instinctively he kicked out and manoeuvred the ball back onto his neck. This time it settled. He took a deep breath in to calm the nerves that had turned to pure adrenaline and then pure dismay. It was fine. A slight wobble. He just couldn't do that again. He'd just have to really wow them. Knowingly, he reached to the shoulders of his Brown's Sporting Goods t-shirt. One last check of the ball. Yes, still stationary. He began to tug. Just an inch at first. As the fabric moved, the ball gently rotated with it. The trick was a tough one to pull off. He had to pull the fabric so cleanly that the ball did not move from its position on his back, but not so slowly that the crowd grew bored. Executed correctly, it never failed to impress. Almost off now. It was halfway over his head. He knew they were transfixed. To them, he seemed totally calm. They didn't know that inside his heart was hammering his ribcage. They didn't know that the thin layer of sweat across his torso was making the move even harder, causing his t-shirt to stick more closely to his chest. Desperately, he willed himself to remain calm. It was almost over. He was almost safe. He'd done this before when he'd been this sweaty. He'd be fine. Most importantly, he couldn't afford to mess up again. Another yank and this time the t-shirt came clean off, the ball remaining in exactly the same spot, held firm by the sweat all around it. A smattering of applause greeted the move and Zak breathed a huge sigh of relief. Just one trick left. He dipped his neck down and then flicked it up, cannoning the ball up in the air before catching it in his hand. 'Tekkers,' he announced to the crowd.

They liked that. They were old and young, mums and dads and footballers and rugby players and people not even interested in sport, applauding warmly. And then there were his friends, the people he knew he could always rely on. Chris and Josh and Marcus; standing together and making most of the noise, screaming with delight and demanding an encore. To their left stood Chloe, more reserved but just as proud. This was for them. That's what Zak told himself as he reached the grand finale, an encore for those watching. Still basking in the applause, he threw the ball up once more and watched its movement carefully. He lifted his head and then cushioned its bounce, expertly stopping it dead still on his forehead. Three seconds. That was the magic number he had to hold it for, to make sure that it had stuck. Yes, there it was. Now for the next part. Carefully, so carefully, he moved his head down so the ball rolled down his nose and stopped on his puckered lips. There it was, the feeling of leather against skin: the most beautiful feeling in the world. He gave it a kiss, as if it was his most precious possession, and then caught it once more before bowing to the crowd.

Recognising his cue, Zak's dad turned the focus of the camera to the crowd as they applauded. 'Nailed it' he mouthed to Zak.

In the moments after his performance, Zak felt as if everything was blurred. All of his nervous tension was released as the crowd shook him by the hand, asked him for selfies, congratulated him.

'Brilliant, just brilliant.' Darren Brown patted Zak enthusiastically on the back before grabbing a microphone. 'Zak performed in the new Panther Sports Hyperlight Performance Range, now available in-store.' He covered the microphone and whispered in Zak's ear. 'Nice one, kiddo. I've never seen anything like it. Stick around for a bit, will you?'

He was getting paid to do this. It seemed beyond belief. As he browsed the shelves and joked about with his mates, he was earning actual money. This was actual work. While Zak wondered just what he should be doing, his dad had positioned himself at the shop front. 'That was @therealTekkerZak performing today,' he told customers as they left the shop, handing them a business card with all of Zak's details on. 'Follow him on social media and keep on supporting Brown's Sporting Goods.' But most of the crowd who had seen him perform had moved on by now, leaving only moderately interested shoppers to distractedly accept the card. They glanced at it, put it in their bag and never looked at it again.

'That's it, the day's over,' Darren Brown announced at 9pm, much to Zak's relief. Once his friends had left, he'd spent the time wandering the shop and examining in detail every single item for sale. He probably knew the Panther Sports range of football boots even better than the Panther Sports owner by now. 'Either make a purchase or scarper,' Darren laughed, half closing the shutters at the front of the shop.

Zak felt Darren's arm around him.

'You've worked absolute wonders for me today, kiddo. I've given your dad the cash, too. I've told him you can have a pair of boots at half price so make sure he sorts that out for you. All I ask in return is a little shout out in your next video.' Darren disappeared into the stock room to do a final count, leaving Zak in the middle of the store. At least all of his wandering around the shop had given him an idea of the boots he wanted. The lime green Panther Sports X10. 'For ultimate playmaking,' read the product description. 'Creativity oozes from the refined leather.' They'd complement his gold boots well. Mainly because they stood out. Sure, he stood out because of his skills but he might as well stand out through his appearance as well.

'Zak Oxden?'

Zak looked around sharply at the sound of the unfamiliar voice. For a moment he looked around in confusion, before his eyes fell upon a man in a flashy leather jacket confidently strolling toward him. With every step his fresh white trainers shone across the scuffed floor of Brown's Sporting Goods. His blue eyes sparkled. His pearl white teeth glistened, a sole golden implant dominating his wide smile. He could have been twenty, but he could have been forty. The truth was hidden by money. The man obviously spent lots on his appearance. His hair had been dyed blond. The teeth had been worked on and the nose was perfectly straight, too straight to be natural. As he stretched out his hand to Zak, the light danced off three golden rings on his fingers. Everything about the man was dazzling, new, fresh. 'Pleasure to meet you.'

'Hello,' Zak said, working up as much energy as he could to smile. He'd been in the shop for a long time and was starting to feel tired.

'It's a pleasure to meet you,' the man said. 'A real pleasure.'

'Erm, thank you.' Zak wondered whether he was going to be asked to pose for a selfie.

'Zak!'

Zak turned to see his dad moving toward him. The man carried on smiling.

'He's a good man, your father.'

'Yes, he is.' Zak looked between his father and the newcomer, wondering if the man was one of the customers his dad had cornered at the entrance. Perhaps they were friends. If that was the case, it was odd that his dad hadn't mentioned it.

'I'm glad to see you two have met.' His dad joined the pair in the centre of the store. 'Zak, meet Tony Curtis.'

Once more, Zak shook the hand of the man in the flash jacket.

'Your father contacted me last week,' Tony explained. 'Cynthia Johnson put him on to me. He said I had to see you in action. Said you're going to be a star. And after today, I know that's the case.'

Zak's spirits soared, his tiredness forgotten. He felt instantly at ease around Tony – the man seemed to have some unseen talent for making people feel special. When he spoke, Zak couldn't help but listen.

'I called in earlier and thought I'd come back when it got a bit quieter. I've already seen your videos of course,' Tony continued. 'They're impressive. Very impressive. We've got an opportunity here.' Tony rubbed his hands together. Zak's dad laughed. A short, sharp burst of happiness.

'Sorry, but who are you?' Zak asked. 'And what do you mean?'

Tony laughed the laugh of a man who rarely has to tell people who he is. It was a laugh of satisfaction with the world. Yes, Tony Curtis was an important man and he would never fail to be surprised when someone didn't know that fact.

'The world, Zak,' Tony replied, ignoring Zak's first question. 'With your talent, you have the potential to make the world sit up and take note. And I have the ability to make that happen.' He looked around at the rows of colourful boots and merchandise.

'That's great,' said Zak. 'But who are you?'

Tony laughed as if the question was outrageous. 'Like your dad said, I'm Tony Curtis.'

'And what do you do?' He wondered if Tony was ever going to give him a straight answer.

'I make people famous. Some people call me an agent but I don't like that word. It makes me seem too shady. I prefer enabler. Because in truth all that I do is find talented people and then enable them to share their talents with the world. To become superstars.'

Zak had read all about agents before. He heard about the vast sums of money they made from moving footballers to new clubs.

'Why do I need an ag—'

'What do you think you could do for Zak?' His dad stopped him mid-sentence. Tony flashed his pearly whites in thanks. He'd been asked to sell himself and selling was his speciality.

'Listen, it's late and I can imagine you're both tired after that brilliant performance. Let's not talk about it here. Why don't the pair of you come to my house tomorrow so we can discuss this properly? What do you say?'

Tomorrow was Saturday and Saturday was football day. 'Zak's got a match in the morning. Why don't we come to your place after that?' his dad suggested. 'Say, 2pm?'

'Sorted.' Tony smiled and held his hand out once more. 'My house is in Kintbury. The one on Oak Lane with the big iron gates, you won't miss it.'

'Isn't that where all of the footballers live?' Zak asked. He'd never been to Kintbury but had heard of it. Tony flashed his smile in Zak's direction.

'There are a few exclusive people in Kintbury, yes. Gated mansion houses, personal bodyguards, you know the score,' he laughed, as if Zak and his dad would ever know the score from living in their two-up, two-down on King's Lane.

'We'll be there,' his dad responded.

Nobody ever turned Tony Curtis down.

YouTube subscribers: 4,597
Instagram followers: 2,701
Twitter followers: 1,142

Zak had never seen such luxury. Tony's house wasn't a house. It was a mansion, tucked away behind vast iron gates and defended by swivelling security cameras. Rooms led on to more rooms, hallways went for what seemed like miles, everything was done to perfection. There was a games room, a cinema, a swimming pool; whatever Zak could think of, Tony owned.

'You could never get bored in this house,' Zak's dad whispered to his son, whose mouth remained wide open.

'Do you like it?' Tony asked, already knowing the answer. A diamond earring caught the sunlight and flashed back at Zak. 'Please do make yourself at home.'

'Thank you, Mr Curtis,' Zak's dad said.

'Please,' Tony laughed. 'Call me Tony.'

'Of course,' he corrected himself. 'Of course.'

'You must be hungry after your game, anyway. How did you get on?'

'We won 4-2,' Zak replied. 'I scored twice.' He felt he needed to add that second part to impress Tony. In truth, the game had been comfortable – another minor obstacle on their way to reclaiming the league title. The league was as good as done. The county cup, however...

'That's great,' Tony replied. 'Come on, let's go into the kitchen and I'll rustle something up. What do you want? Pizza? Chicken pasta? I know what you footballers are like.'

When Tony said that he'd rustle something up, what he meant was that he'd get someone else to rustle it up for him. Both options sounded good, but in the end Zak opted for chicken pasta. Mr Jones would approve of such a healthy choice, he thought. Right away Tony hit a buzzer and a man came running. 'Three chicken pastas, please,' Tony said. 'How about that special recipe you make it with?' The man nodded and turned on his heel. 'The food will be ready in thirty minutes,' Tony announced. 'While we wait, I'd like to show you something.'

He led Zak and his dad down another hallway and into a room they hadn't yet visited. The walls were covered with photographs. Moments from Tony's life, all frozen in time. There was Tony shaking hands with famous people, Tony at football stadiums in the most expensive seats, with musicians, film stars, people Zak didn't recognise. Each time dressed immaculately. Each time dazzling with his jewellery and his sparkle and his natural confidence.

'Is that Messi?' Zak stood open-mouthed in front of a photo of Tony at Barcelona's Camp Nou stadium, his arm around a small footballer with brown, floppy hair.

'I call him Lionel,' Tony smiled. 'But yes, that is him. We're good friends.'

'Wow.' Maybe Tony was the real deal. He couldn't just be any old agent to be friends with the best player the world has ever seen.

'There's one thing that links all of them,' Tony said, nodding toward the photos. 'All of the people in these pictures are different. They look different. They sound different. But really they're the same. And now I'm not just talking about the pictures. I'm talking about everybody on this planet. We're all the same. We all want to be somebody. To be famous.'

'Now not all of these clients are mine,' Tony continued. 'I haven't enabled all of them to get to where they are. But I've helped many. Again, please don't call me their agent. I'm their enabler. You might recognise this one?'

Zak would recognise that messy blond hair anywhere. Even in pictures the figure radiated energy. Just like he did in all of the videos that Zak had studied so carefully.

'Baller B came to me when he had little more than 1,000 followers,' Tony explained. 'And I saw an opportunity. Look at him now. Millions of followers. His own clothing range. Millions of pounds of income. That could be you.'

Any doubt that Zak had about having an agent were quickly disappearing. Earlier that morning he'd been unsure if he needed Tony. He'd been doing okay by himself, hadn't he? But then he saw the house and had been blown away by such riches. And now this, the cherry on top of the grand cake Tony was offering.

'And he's just one of many who came to me wanting to find fame,' Tony continued. 'Some of them as sports stars. Others as celebrities. And more recently, many of them online. It's simple really. They come to me with their talent. I do the rest.'

The sound of steel drums blared from Tony's pocket. He checked his phone and suddenly his face lit up. 'Perfect! Just perfect!' he screamed, sliding across the screen to answer. 'B! How are you doing, dude . . . yes, yes. Listen, I'll call you back later. First, I've got someone I want you to speak to . . . yes . . . no . . . he's going to be the real deal. Okay, cool.' He handed Zak his phone. 'It's Baller B. He just wants to say hello.' Zak reached out with a clammy palm. The day before he'd been a freestyler. Now he was speaking to one of the biggest in the game.

'Hello,' he murmured. Idiot. Superstar YouTubers wouldn't say hello. They'd say yo or easy or what's up.

'What's up,' came the reply, the same voice that he'd heard on those videos, slightly high-pitched yet always excitable. 'Tony tells me you're going to be a star. He's a top guy. Never led me wrong once.'

'Okay.' This was even more nerve-wracking than his performance in front of all of those people. Messing up again would be unforgivable. You only get one chance to make a first impression.

'Pass it back, Zak,' Tony motioned with his hand and he returned the phone with relief. A series of diamonds flashed back at him from the phone case. He'd just been holding something more valuable than all of the items in their house on King's Lane.

'Later then, B.' Tony put the phone back in his pocket. 'So, where was I? Yes, of course. Your situation. I'm sure you've guessed by now but I'd like to enable you, too. I work in an informal manner. There are no contracts. Contracts are old-school. I'm all about the future. There are lots of people I'd like to introduce to you. I'm pals with the heads of content at Facebook and YouTube. When I give them the word, they can flick the switch and make sure that your videos are seen by millions instead of thousands. I know the best editors in the game. I like what you're doing and Dean, you're golden, but to get to the next level we need the very best videographers and editors. I can take you to a life you never thought imaginable. I can picture it now. TekkerZak merchandise. Live performances. Millions of followers. Gold plaques from YouTube. More brand deals than you can imagine. The money will be pouring in. Your dad won't ever have to worry about getting another day's building work in his life. And all I ask is for 25% of whatever money I bring you in. A one-time offer.'

Zak felt his dad's eyes on him. He felt Tony's eyes on him. He could barely feel his own eyes, they'd popped so far out of his head. He was doing fine before. But he'd be doing more than fine after if he said yes. He pictured the pupils of Redwood Community College wearing his merchandise, his own mansion, his own phone with diamonds in the case, his dad never having to worry about working again.

Tony was right. Everybody did want to be famous and Zak realised that he was no different. He'd always thought of himself as a famous footballer, scoring match-winning goals on the biggest stage, representing his country, sending millions of fans around the world into delirium with his skills. More recently, however, his dream had changed. He'd be famous, but not as a professional footballer. The internet had opened up a whole new world. Where once Zak imagined goals, he now imagined insane tricks. Fans became followers. Goals became likes. There was no doubt about it; Zak wanted to be a famous online personality. What was there to lose? They'd made £200 so far. Tony wasn't asking for any more. All he wanted was a percentage of the money he brought in. There was no bad outcome.

'I'll go check on the chicken. Speak it through in private then meet me in the dining room in a couple of minutes.'

'Thank you, Mr Curtis,' his dad replied.

'Remember, call me Tony.'

'Of course,' Zak's dad corrected himself again. 'Of course. Sometimes I just get carried away.'

'That's quite all right. I'm going to make a phone call anyway. Take as long as you like. They can always keep the meal warm for you.'

As soon as the door closed in a flash of diamond and Tony was gone, Zak started speaking. Immediately.

'It sounds amazing, Dad!'

'Yes, yes it does, son,' his dad replied, smiling. 'I was told that Mr Curtis is the best in the business. Part of me wonders if it's all a little too good to be true. I'm a bit uneasy about there being no contract. That's one of my requirements. Do you have any?' Zak's inside plummeted. What could his dad possibly be unsure about? If only he opened his eyes he'd see the riches all around him. How could Tony be lying? He shook his head. Anything to get his dad to accept the offer. The details didn't even matter to him. The two of them could deal with the paperwork. He just wanted to make videos and become a star, no matter how it happened.

'I've never wanted anything more in my life.' Zak meant it, too.

'That's great. I need to know how long he plans to represent you for too. What his first plans are. If there are any insurance policies he has planned. Once that's all made clear, I think we should go for it.' Inside Zak screamed. Outside Zak screamed, opening his mouth without realising.

'Yes!'

'Yes?'

'Yes,' he repeated, more calmly this time.

Tony sat waiting for them in the dining room, his pearly white teeth reflecting the sunlight that streamed in through the open window. A mouth-watering smell of fresh chicken floated in from the kitchen next door, reminding Zak of just how hungry he was. He couldn't wait to eat. Could they just wrap the deal up right now?

'Have we got ourselves an agreement then?' he winked.

The pair of them should have known that Tony Curtis always gets what Tony Curtis wants. Within two minutes his dad's questions had been batted away and answered for like they were minor inconveniences. There was nothing left to decide, other than to make it official.

Zak had an agent.

No, an *enabler*.

YouTube subscribers: 22,882
Instagram followers: 12,096
Twitter followers: 2,704

The next few days were a whirlwind. Tony was true to his word. He could make things happen. And if they carried on happening, Zak was sure that he would become a star.

Zak now had his own agent. He also had his own video editor. Tony had suggested an editor called Jazz with pink spiky hair and two nose rings that worked with a number of his most high-profile clients. Zak and his dad both approved. She knew the right backing tracks to add, dubbed over sounds seamlessly and made everything much smoother. She was joined by a videographer called Nat, his whole body covered in tattoos, his movements jerky but his camera work steady. Crucially, Nat had the very best technology to shoot with. Zak would look so good on his videos that his viewers would feel like they could jump into the screen and stand alongside him. Phone calls were made to all of the social media sites. Instagram instantly agreed to highlight his videos on the explore section to all relevant users. YouTube selected him as a featured creator. With the work he'd previously done now being covered, his dad took on the official role of manager. What this involved, neither of them knew. Still he hoped for work each day but it was no longer essential. The first paycheque had come through from YouTube and Facebook for views. £1,496. It wasn't massive but it was a start. And it would at least mean that some of the bills that littered the kitchen table would disappear.

The first video of the new era was a cut from Zak's two-minute performance at Brown's Sporting Goods. Jazz chose 'I Wonder' by Kanye West as the backing track. Tony wanted Zac to act like he was already a star and the lyrics fitted perfectly. Jazz looped one of the lines – *I'm a star how could I not shine* – over and over at the start of the video, introducing the new Zak to the world. With the right level of zoom and effects, she then made it appear as if Zak had performed in front of hundreds who had all rushed to him as soon as he was finished. It looked so realistic that Zak even began to wonder if that was how things had really happened.

It was no surprise when the video was Zak's most successful yet.

In just 24 hours it received 50,000 views.

The subscriber count on Zak's channel kept on going up. More people were stumbling across his videos and liking what they saw. And some of those people were influential themselves.

Baller B, Z2K and ItsMintThat all followed Zak. They were

clients of Tony's and were all officially verified by their social media platforms. The blue tick that displayed proudly next to their names was the closest anyone could get to online royalty. Tony assured Zak that it was only a matter of time before he received a blue tick of his very own.

'What we need first, though,' Tony told him, 'is to increase your visibility.'

'You're absolutely right, Mr Curtis,' Zak's dad replied automatically. In just a few short days Tony had earned his faith. Any questions about contracts and insurance were long forgotten.

'You've made a great start with your online content, but now we need to get you some more appearances. I'm talking media, other online talents, events.'

It all made sense to Zak. His dad was positively beaming.

'It's only a matter of time before we make it big,' he repeated over and over.

As far as Zak's mates were concerned, he'd already made it big. In the corridors of Redwood Community College he was asked for selfies by even more people that he'd never seen before and didn't know. Encouraged by Chris, the oldest kids in the school greeted him personally. Teachers said hello and congratulated him. Wherever he walked, he left a buzz of excitement in his footsteps. Even the three hulking trolls who had chased him left him alone. It was as if he could do no wrong. And it was just the same at Redwood Rovers. When he turned up for training a hush descended over the group. They'd all seen his performance at Brown's Sporting Goods, either online or in person. Even Mr Jones seemed mildly impressed.

'Let's hope you show such command of the ball in the game this weekend.' He winked at Zak.

'Zak, you know I thought that was nuts.' Chris ran up beside him during the lap around the pitch Mr Jones had sent them on to warm up. 'But when I watched that video it was like I was watching the F2 Freestylers on Redwood High Street!'

'If you keep doing that they'll have to make it the F3,' Josh observed. 'Imagine that: Billy, Jez and Zak as the ultimate team of freestylers!'

'Pfft, Zak's better than them,' Marcus laughed.

Such compliments were becoming increasingly common. Zak had never felt such confidence – and it was showing on the pitch. He manoeuvred the ball with ease. Everything felt so much simpler. It was as if the goal was bigger, his opponents smaller, the pitch flatter. He barely had to think as he nutmegged Josh, then stopped the ball, turned and rainbow flicked the ball back over him. Everything came naturally. Marcus dived at him and he flip-flapped, swerving outside then inside, the ball stuck to his feet. Just the keeper now. Zak approached not just with the intention to wrong foot her, but to embarrass her. If he could pull it off in training he could do it in a match. And if he did it in a match it'd look sick. Another touch forward brought her out from her goal. Closer, he needed her five yards away. Fran was fearless. That was why Mr Jones chose her as his main keeper. But her strength had become her weakness. She took the bait. Zak eyed his spot in the goal and then thrashed his foot forward. Fran second guessed him and dived to her right, exactly where Zak had been looking. Powerfully, his foot followed through with all of the force he could muster. But the ball didn't. Because he hadn't been aiming at the ball. He'd wanted to fake the whole thing. Too late, Fran realised she'd been tricked. Nonchalantly, Zak rolled the ball into the empty net for his fifth goal of the training match. That was enough for Mr Jones, who blew his whistle to signal the end of the session.

'Good work,' he announced, which was as much of a compliment as any team of his could ever expect to receive. 'Let's take that into the weekend's game.'

The last 16 of the county cup. Zak had never felt more ready for a football game. But first he had the small matter of his second ever public freestyle appearance, organised by Tony at Redwood Shopping Centre as a way of increasing his visibility and engaging with his fans on a personal level. A few weeks ago Zak would have found that sentence ridiculous, but to the new Zak it made so much sense. Especially because he was being paid £500 for it.

Time moved painfully slowly the next day at school. Zak found himself checking the clock on the wall of the classroom every five minutes. All of his kit was in a bag in his locker. He'd brought it all to school so that he could go straight to the shopping centre and warm up before performing at 5pm. Tony would meet him at 4pm by the John Lewis superstore. School, he felt, was the only thing in his life right now that wasn't exciting. If it wasn't for school, he'd spend his time going from one buzz to another, his whole world a constant cycle of thrills. Lucky he had a whole team behind him now. While he was sitting in maths with Mrs Parnell, Nat was editing the latest video that he'd shot – a series of groundwork moves featuring blurred reverse stepovers, knee akkas, fakies and triangles. She'd then hit the publish button at 3pm to make sure thousands of viewers watched it just after their school day finished. Including Zak.

If y is 15, what is x? Zak studied the question, wracked his brains, then glanced a look at his neighbour's sheet to see what she'd put. It was easier that way. No sooner had he written 3.5 than the bell had gone. Finally. Lunchtime. Four lessons down, two to go. In the chaos of bags and movement that always came with the bell, he sneaked a glance at his phone. One new message from Jazz. She had the video ready. Moving the phone under the table so that it was out of Mrs Parnell's sight, he clicked play on the video she had sent.

A series of rolls and jumps, all in time to the beat Jazz had put on the track, 'Superstar' by Lupe Fiasco. Good choice, he reflected. Then the on-screen Zak was down, stopping the ball with his knee and then shifting his weight forward and pressing the ball down so that it flew up over his head. Yes, his followers would like that one. She'd put the akka on last, followed by his trademark 'tekkers' shout. He sent her back the okay emoji. As long as the video got Tony's seal of approval, it'd go live.

The others had already started the game by the time he joined them on the playground. They were playing against the year 9s with a tennis ball, one goal marked on the wall, the other by blazers. The small green ball fizzed around the concrete, no fewer than forty pupils involved in the game.

'Come help us out, Zak,' Chloe shouted over to him. 'We're 6-3 down.'

'I don't know how, the year 9s are awful,' Chris shouted over. A particularly burly year 9 took offence and motioned for his friend to come over. Together they picked Chris up and dropped him into one of the open bins on the playground. Zak did his best not to laugh.

'Don't worry about that,' Chloe added, pointing over at Chris. 'He'll only tell us later that he bashed them up and put *them* in the bin. And we'll let you off being late as long as you aren't late tonight.'

There was no way that Zak would be late tonight. He charged around the playground like a man possessed. There was added pressure on him now. Everyone in the school knew about his videos and they expected him to be just as skilful whenever they saw him in action. He demanded the ball from his friends, then dipped and dived and ducked and swerved around the year 9s. They couldn't catch him. These days Zak felt that nobody could catch him. By the time the bell rang, the year 8s were 12-10 up.

'Nice one,' Chloe said, jogging over to him a little breathlessly. 'Shame you couldn't score as many as me. So what time shall we pick you up tonight?'

'Don't worry,' Zak replied, ignoring the fact that Chloe had scored more goals than him. He could let her have that one. 'I'm walking there after school.' Chloe raised both eyebrows at Zak.

'You're walking twenty miles?' What was she on about?

'No, it's about a twenty-minute walk to the shopping centre.'

'The concert isn't at the shopping centre,' Chloe shot back. Something was wrong here. 'And there's no way that you'd be able to walk all the way to High Grove.' Ten seconds passed by, Chloe staring accusingly at Zak and Zak doing his best to figure out what she was talking about. And then it came to him. The concert. Yes, it was coming back now. He had agreed to go to the Peakz concert with her. They both loved listening to Peakz. But was that really tonight? So much had gone on since then it was as if his memory had been wiped.

'Chloe,' he emphasised every letter in his most apologetic voice. 'I'm so sorry. I can't come. Tony has organised an event and I have to go.'

If looks could kill, Zak would have long been dead. Chloe's eyes shot daggers in his direction, her brow furrowed.

'Oh right,' she said primly, trying and failing to hold her anger in. 'And what's so important about this event that you have to let down your best mate?'

'Well it's at Redwood Shopping Centre and Tony says it's important for me to engage with my fans. And they're paying me £500!' Even before that last sentence, Zak could tell that he was only digging himself into a deeper hole. He wished the playground could open him up and swallow him whole. Anything to get him out of the situation. He hated to let his best mate down. But he'd really hate to let Tony down.

'Your fans!' Chloe had to hold back a laugh. Not a 'ha ha' laugh but something much darker. 'Come on, Zak. Okay, a few people turned up to Brown's the other day but I'm not sure you can call them your fans.'

Now it was Zak's turn to raise his voice. Yes, he'd let her down and he felt terrible, but couldn't she be happy for him? He frowned, a steely look of displeasure. Then he raised himself up to his full height, drawing his shoulders forward and his chest out and snapped back at her. 'I've got thousands of fans. Just look at my social media followers.'

'Yeah, but what does that mean? How do you know your followers even exist? They could be fake accounts or bots or old men pretending to be little girls.'

'They're real.'

'Sure.' The pair held their ground on the rapidly emptying playground. Neither was willing to break off their glare. Ten seconds, twenty. The next lesson would soon be starting. And then Chloe broke.

'So you're not coming tonight, no?' Chloe asked.

'I'm sorry, Chloe. I can't.'

'Fine.'

Her tone made it clear it was definitely *not* fine.

'I'm sorry.'

'No, it's fine. If that's what you want. I'll go and see if Chris has found his way out of the bin yet and invite him. But just listen to you. All this talk of fans and social media and likes and views. Don't lose track of what's real. And don't be disappointed when only four of your *fans* turn up to watch you.' She spat out the word fans and then marched off the playground, hurrying along to her next lesson. Zak shrugged. Let her moan. He didn't care what she thought. He could do just fine without her.

If time had been going slowly that morning, it seemed to be going backwards that afternoon. Zak could have sworn that at one point the clock went from 2.50pm to 2.40pm. It was hot inside the classroom, a perfect spring afternoon, and the floor-to-ceiling glass windows only made it hotter. For the thirty pupils inside, it was like being cooked in a greenhouse. For the assistant headteacher, Mr Davies, however, there was no reason to open any of the windows. Maybe it's because he's got a heart of stone, Zak thought. In the heat his mind drifted, thinking back to his argument with Chloe. Tony had told him that to become a star he'd have to make sacrifices, but he didn't think he'd have to make them this soon. Could he really sacrifice his best mate? Then he thought back to her horrible glance, her accusing look and thought that maybe he could. People grow and move on, don't they? Maybe he'd just outgrown her. 'In the mid-eighteenth century, the Industrial Revolution took hold of Europe.' Mr Davies's voice zoned in and out of his consciousness. 'Inventions such as the spinning jenny and the water frame drastically reduced the production time needed for materials.' Always new inventions. Always new trends. Zak stole another look at the clock. 3:01pm. His video! Zak waited until Mr Davies turned to the interactive whiteboard and then swooped for the phone in his pocket. 'There are some activities in the textbooks in front of you that I'd like you carry out for the final twenty minutes,' he heard. Quickly, Zak glanced up. Mr Davies still had his head turned to the board. There was time. The red and white homepage bounced up onto the page and Zak saw the video safely uploaded. He looked on with pride, just as he always did when he saw his videos out in public for the first time.

1,486 views already.

Mad.

He locked the phone and slipped it back into his pocket just as Mr Davies turned his head. 'Off you go.' There wasn't long left in the day now. Zak had waited long enough to be free. He could wait another twenty minutes. The textbook in front of him was dense and the pages caught in his fingers as he flicked back and forth until landing on the page Mr Davies wanted him to be on. Maybe three centuries from now pupils would learn about the digital revolution. They'd be taught about the internet and social media and maybe even YouTube.

1a) What was made compulsory by the 1833 Factory Act?

He scanned the page before seeing the answer. *The 1833 Factory Act was passed by the government to improve working conditions for children. It stipulated that no children under the age of nine could work. Children between the ages of 9-13 could work no longer than nine hours a day. Children aged 13-18 could work no longer than twelve hours a day. All children must have two hours of schooling per day.* Alongside the answer there was a black and white sketch of children working great lumbersome machines under the brutal watch of a balding adult. He shook his head. How had that ever been allowed to happen?

Onto the next question.

1b) In what way did 'roof and pillar' work improve coal mining?

Zak looked again at the clock. 3:13pm. Suddenly his pocket felt red hot. It had been more than ten minutes since he last checked his video! Any concentration that had been on the textbook was gone in an instant. It was taking all of his effort not to reach into his pocket. All around him, his classmates worked in silence, just how Mr Davies liked it. Mr Davies himself sat at the front of the classroom marking exercise books. He was methodical in his work, taking one book, crossing and ticking (but mainly crossing), then taking the next book. It was as if the books were on a conveyor belt in his own factory. This was his chance. Quickly, he reached for his phone, keeping it safely underneath the table to hide it from view. He swiped up to unlock, then pulled down on the screen to refresh. His heart nearly leapt from his body. 3,764 views. They'd more than doubled in just over ten minutes! He wanted to jump from his desk and dance around the classroom, he wanted to sing at the top of his—

'Oxden! What are you doing?' Thirty heads turned to look at Zak. Mr Davies stood up from his desk and paced toward him. Blood flushed to his face. Nobody dared disobey the rules when Mr Davies was teaching! Zak felt like a rabbit trapped in headlights. He dropped the phone to the floor and held up both hands. 'Nothing, sir.'

'What's that on the floor?' This was looking dangerous. Desperately, Zak shifted his trainers that should have been school shoes on top of the phone, then looked down.

'I can't see anything, s—'

'It's a phone, Oxden!' Mr Davies cut him off. He'd been around long enough to see all of the tricks of the trade. Nobody would fool him. 'Hand it over,' he demanded.

'Hand over what?' Zak asked. Mr Davies's nostrils flared in anger, his black nostril hairs swinging back and forth.

'I will not tolerate liars. Hand over the phone now or you'll be in deep trouble.' Zak assessed his options. He could hand over the phone and be in deep trouble. Or he could not hand over the phone and be in *really* deep trouble. Thirty pairs of eyes watched as he begrudgingly bent down and picked his phone up off the floor.

'This will stay with me,' Mr Davies announced. 'You can

collect it at the end of the lesson. And then you can stay with me after school.' He shook his head. 'I don't know why you kids insist on using your phones in school.'

'But sir! I've got to leave on time today, I've got a big event.'

Mr Davies grinned. 'You should have thought about that before you broke the rules.'

'Go on sir,' Josh chimed in. 'Let him off.'

'Yeah, sir,' Marcus added.

'Silence!' Mr Davies's voice cut the atmosphere. 'I will have silent working. Textbooks open, answer your questions. The next person to say a word will join Zak in my office.'

Thirty heads immediately reverted to their textbooks, including Zak's. What had he done? His mind was racing, the words all appearing blurred in front of him. He couldn't take them in. He'd been stupid, so stupid. And now he was trapped.

YouTube subscribers: 24,622
Instagram followers: 12,998
Twitter followers: 2,991

Mr Davies led Zak down the labyrinth of corridors that made up Redwood Community College. All around him pupils laughed and shouted as they left school for the day, happy at the long evenings that lay ahead. 'Erm, how long will this take?' Zak asked.

'As long as I want,' Mr Davies replied curtly. 'On your phone in a lesson. Who do you think you are?'

The best response, Zak realised, was to remain silent. He had to do whatever Mr Davies asked. Anything to be let out as quickly as possible. Mr Davies opened the door to his office and nodded to the empty chair, inviting Zak to sit. A faint smell of coffee escaped from the room, which was just as bare as before. Inside there was no sign of emotion or personality.

Zak wondered if Mr Davies had a family. There were no pictures of them if he did. There were no pictures of anything. Just textbooks and folders and certificates. The room of a man whose life revolved around the school.

Mr Davies reached out for a textbook. *History: Complete Revision and Practice.* 'Because you appear to have nothing better to do in my lessons, you can learn the syllabus all over again.'

'Don't you have anything better to do after school?' Zak shot back. Mr Davies wasn't joking. He could ruin everything.

'I can wait as long as I want,' he replied. 'Whereas you seemingly can't.'

'You're right, sir. I've got a really important event. Honest. I can call my dad and he'll tell you everything. Please let me out. I'll do detention any other day.' Zak changed his approach. He was desperate. He'd get down on his knees and lick Mr Davies's shoes if that's what it took.

'Chapter eight,' Mr Davies replied coldly. 'I want you to copy it out by hand. Once that's done you'll be free to go.' The floor opened up and swallowed Zak. His insides plummeted faster than a stone in water.

'But sir—'

'I suggest you start now.'

Defeated, Zak turned to chapter eight: The Industrial Revolution in England. There were fifteen pages. It'd take forever. There was no way he'd finish in time! He hated Mr Davies. Truly detested him. The worst thing was, Mr Davies seemed to take joy in Zak's pain.

How could he get out of it?

He could fake an illness. Mr Davies wouldn't want to deal with someone who had diarrhoea. No, that wouldn't work. Mr Davies would wait for him outside the bathroom. Could he make a run for it? Maybe. But then how would he get his phone out of the locked drawer in the classroom? He'd be naked without it. He felt Mr Davies's eyes on him. He looked up and sure enough, Mr Davies was staring at him. Zak started to copy down the words from the textbook. He worked quickly, the pen furiously scratching against the lined paper. That satisfied Mr Davies, who went back to reading his book.

The tick of the clock punctuated every second, loudly reminding Zak of his time that was fast disappearing. 3:45. If he left now he could just about run and meet Tony in time. 3:55. Too late. His wrist was beginning to hurt. He'd written three sides of A4, covering six pages of the textbook. Almost halfway there. He willed his wrist to keep going. This was torture. How could teachers be allowed to do this still? Mr Davies seemed more content than Zak had ever seen him, sitting back in his chair and reading his book as if he had no care in the world.

'Right, Oxden. That'll do,' Mr Davies announced with Zak copying down a section on the 1844 Railway Regulation Act. 'I hope you've learned your lesson.'

'Yes, sir.' Zak's words gushed out of him. 'Promise, sir. Definitely, sir.'

'Good. Off you go, then.' Mr Davies nodded gently in the direction of the door. 'Get out of my sight.'

'But my phone, sir!' Zak protested. Mr Davies's lips twitched into the faintest sign of a smile.

'Oh, yes. Your phone. Here.' He passed Zak the phone. It

hadn't been in his drawer. It had been in his pocket the whole time. Lucky he hadn't made a run for it! But now he really did have to make a run for it. He swept out of the room in record pace and sprinted toward his locker. 4:25. He still had time to get there. He'd just miss the chance to warm up. That was fine. He could go straight into his routine. He could do anything.

His phone buzzed angrily and Zak looked at the screen. Tony Curtis. Hurriedly, he answered it.

'Where are you?' the voice was cold and demanding. Nobody made Tony Curtis wait.

'I'm . . . at . . . school,' he'd reached the locker by now and rammed his metal key into the lock. His bags came tumbling out. 'I was given detention but I'm done now. I'm coming. Promise.'

'Didn't they know you had an event!' Tony sounded outraged.

'I told them and they didn't listen.'

'Ridiculous. Ridiculous. This is the problem with schools,' Tony muttered. 'Well, we'll have to cope. Wait at the entrance. I'll pick you up in ten minutes.'

YouTube subscribers: 32,232
Instagram followers: 19,324
Twitter followers: 3,124

Groups of hooded teenagers hung about on the corners of the Redwood Shopping Centre, content with not really doing much. Couples held hands and blocked the walkways. Pretzel pop-ups handed out free samples. Families moved too slowly. Music blared from the shopfronts, while perfume drifted through the stale air. Distractions were everywhere. All around them, humanity buzzed.

A small area had been kept open for Zak. Advertising boards with Redwood Shopping Centre's logo stood behind him. In front lay the food court, full of staff preparing for the evening onrush. 'How long have I got?' Zak asked. Tony had broken all of the speed limits to get there in time. Fortunately, his BMW i8 was more than capable of accelerating at speed, its

1.5-litre, three-cylinder engine able to go from 0-60 miles per hour in four seconds. Zak threw on his kit in the car, doing his best to stay upright as Tony swerved around various obstacles. They'd been greeted by a smiling lady in smart dress, Harriette, who introduced herself as the shopping centre manager. 'We've already got a crowd gathering,' she had announced.

Harriette, it turned out, had a different definition of a crowd to Zak and Tony. Despite his dad doing his best to drum up interest by handing out business cards, just three mildly interested ladies lingered around the hastily put-together area for Zak.

Tony checked his Rolex watch. 'Five minutes,' he told Zak. 'You'll be fine.'

Another two people joined the crowd, both of them teenagers. 'I think you'll like what we've done here,' Harriette said as she passed Zak his ball. 'Look!' Redwood Shopping Centre logos covered the ball's cheap plastic. It didn't feel properly pumped up but it'd have to do.

'Can I practise?'

'Oh, no,' Harriette replied. 'We need some pictures of you. Before you get too sweaty of course,' she smiled a sickly-sweet smile. 'Can you stand in front of the board?'

Zak moved five paces to his left so he was dead in front of the board, urging Harriette to hurry up. He'd planned a complex routine for the crowd. But without a warm-up, he'd struggle to nail it. 'Say cheese!' Harriette announced, holding up her iPhone XS. Zak smiled, showing plenty of teeth. Inside he may have been feeling frustrated, impatient and even slightly nervous, but outside he had to be the picture of calm. After all, wasn't that what being a YouTuber was about? Appearances . . .

'And now, upstairs by the food court, we have superstar freestyler Tekkers Dan!' the notice from the tannoy rang out over the hubbub. Zak winced. Had they really called him Dan? 'Get there now. He'll be starting in two minutes. That's two minutes folks!'

'A few more!' Harriette insisted. 'And then I need a video of you saying 'I shop at Redwood Shopping Centre.' Can you do that for me?'

'I shop at Redwood Shopping Centre!' Zak said as directed. Time was slipping away.

'Once more!' Harriette chimed. Tony stood behind her with his thumb up and his bicep tensed. 'That's golden,' he commented, a flash of teeth reflecting the artificial light.

'Okay, I'm going to stay on the side so I can film you,' Harriette announced. 'If you can start in one minute that will be fantastic. Make it five minutes and then hang around so you can freestyle with our shoppers. Perfect!'

Finally, Zak was left with the ball. Finally, after all of this time, his moment had come. There was Harriette and Tony and his dad and also Nat, waiting expectantly with his chunky camera. And then there was the crowd. All five of them.

Surely that couldn't be right?

Five people. But he had *tens of thousands* of fans.

'And here he is, ladies and gentlemen, Tekkerz Dan!' A dance track that Zak didn't recognise boomed from the speakers all over the shopping centre, drowning out the tracks coming from the individual shops. How could they not know his name? Well, he'd make sure they all knew his name after this performance.

Showtime.

A hocus pocus to start. Zak shifted his left foot forward and then dragged the ball across his body behind his front foot, then shifted the angle of the foot so the ball deflected forward. With his front foot he then jumped, landing with both feet on top of the ball. Now he was standing on the ball and he lifted his right hand above his eyes as if to playfully look out to the crowd. There were six of them now. Seven if you included the dog. Why was there a dog in the shopping centre? That was Zak's main thought as the ball went from under him. Everything was upright, and then everything was sideways. As the ball rolled to the side, Zak fell where he had just been standing. Nobody had been expecting it, least of all Zak. He crashed onto the unforgiving floor of the food court. Pain shot into his left knee, which had taken most of the weight from the fall. His eyes began to water. No. He had to get up. He had to carry on the routine. Wiping his eyes before anyone could notice, Zak retrieved the ball and stood on it once more, this time pulling off the move. Still standing on the ball, he turned his entire body and the ball ninety degrees, then again, four times until he was back in exactly the same spot. Lukewarm applause came from the crowd. He was winning them back. But wait. The two teenagers had wandered off. Why would they do that?

He'd have to pull off something special. Zak bent down and smacked the plastic ball into the instep of his left trainer, shooting it up into the air. He then turned and caught it between his heel and bum. Just as soon as it had nestled, the ball was out again, kicked up by the heel of his standing foot. That was better. He leant back and allowed the ball to come to a rest on his chest, then dropped all the way to the ground so that he was lying on his back, the ball still on his chest. He puffed his chest up and his belly down then popped his belly up so the ball rose sharply. He raised his feet in expectation but the ball never came. He hadn't popped it up enough! This was useless. What was the point? He was embarrassing himself and even if he had nailed the routine, he'd be embarrassing himself. After all, barely anybody was watching him. Every part of him wanted to walk off, but then he thought of what would happen if he did. And so resigned, he chased after the ball once more.

By the end of the routine, the crowd was down to four people. The applause were once more lukewarm. Jazz would have to work hard on that edit, Zak thought. He'd been terrible. And no wonder with the preparation. At least he had that to blame it on. And at least the fact that there was hardly any crowd meant he didn't have to hang around. Within ten minutes they'd disappeared, willing only to have a few passes back and forth. His dad succeeded in flagging down a few more shoppers for a touch of freestyling, but that was all. Even the ever-enthusiastic Harriette admitted it was best to call it a day after thirty minutes of waiting.

'Not to worry,' Tony reassured them, his teeth glimmering with every word. 'You might have messed up but you still get the money. And anyway, we're aiming for the world. We don't want you to be stuck in Redwood for your whole life. With a bit of editorial work we can make it look like you knocked it out of the park.'

Zak was sure that Jazz could work her magic on the edit. Still, the event had been a disappointment. A setback on the road to stardom. And maybe, just maybe, a reality check.

YouTube subscribers: 33,799
Instagram followers: 20,824
Twitter followers: 3,613

Tony had told Zak not to worry. Zak did worry, though. He worried that he'd never be asked to perform live at an event again. He worried that the few people who had watched him would tell others of how he'd messed up. Even worse, he worried that the video of him falling over would go viral. He'd be finished.

That morning he'd been so worried he couldn't even face going to school. For once, his dad allowed him to phone in sick. 'Take today off,' he had said. 'Get your mind right and promise me you'll give 110% effort in your lessons on Monday.' Zak wasn't in a state to promise anything. He just wanted to be left alone in bed. But still he nodded back at his dad.

By lunchtime, however, Zak was restless. He'd spent the

whole morning interacting with his fans on social media, doing his best to grow his follower numbers to get over the disappointment of the night before. For every person who commented #instasquad, he liked a post of theirs. That way they'd be more likely to convert from a fan of his to a superfan. Having more superfans would mean that his work would be shared more widely, would be talked about in playgrounds up and down the country just like Baller B's videos. If he had more followers, he'd be more likely to get work with big brands and businesses, which would then get him even more followers. He might even have more than five people turn up to see him perform. The whole thing was a beautiful cycle, at least in theory.

'Mr Curtis! How are you?' his dad's voice drifted through the floorboards. 'What's that? Sure, he's just up in his room. No, he didn't go to school today. He didn't feel well. Let me go up and get him.' Zak jumped out of bed and raced onto the landing, meeting his dad halfway up the stairs.

'Zed Dog!' Tony hollered into the line. Zak winced at the sound of the nickname Tony had given him. No-one had asked him if he even wanted a nickname, but he'd decided it'd be wise to let Tony do as he pleased for now. Especially if he could make him a star.

'Hi, Tony. How you doing?'

'Good, good, good. Good. Listen, I'm going to say two words. I've said them before to you but I'll say them again: Baller B. What you thinking?'

Fame. Fortune. Followers. In many ways Baller B had it all. And yet in many ways he didn't. Zak thoughts his skills average at best. His understanding of football not amazing. But Zak didn't want to get into a debate about that with Tony, not when Baller B was a client of his.

'He's sick,' Zak replied, knowing that was exactly what Tony wanted to hear.

'So this is what I'm thinking. Baller B and Zak Oxden's ultimate football challenges. We're talking crossbar challenges, penalty shootouts, who can hit top bins the most? Public nutmegs: one minute to try and put the ball through as many people's legs as possible. One v one games of *FIFA*, best of five, live streamed to all of your followers. It makes sense. Baller B's fans see your skills and follow you if they don't already. Amazing visibility. Baller B introduces a fresh new talent. Amazing credibility. It's the starts of a beautiful new partnership. What do you reckon?'

'Do you mean I'll film a video with Baller B?' Zak couldn't help but hide his excitement.

'Film it? You'll star in it, Zed Dog!'

It was all arranged with alarming quickness. Ideas excited Tony. As soon as they came to him, he had to bring them to life as quickly as possible. Especially when they'd help to banish the memory of the shopping centre. That very afternoon, Tony phoned Baller B and got his agreement. Within an hour of his first phone call to Zak, the house phone rang once more. Zak raced to answer it, desperate for news. It didn't matter that Baller B's skills weren't great, that his understanding of football wasn't the best. Everyone had heard of Baller B. And if everyone had heard of Baller B, did that mean that everyone would soon hear of Zak?

'He's in,' Tony announced. He didn't even bother to say hello. Too many words. Waves of excitement crashed through Zak's body. He was going to shoot a video with Baller B. He'd beat him at the crossbar challenge, no doubt. He'd show the world his skills.

'He's a wicked guy.' Tony's words brought Zak's attention back to the phone. 'I've already run the idea past him and he's hugely excited for it. We've already arranged it for Saturday late morning. Be at Upper Street Rec, 11am.'

Saturday.

The match.

The waves of excitement became jolts of anxiety. Zak couldn't miss the match. He'd never missed a Redwood match, not even the time he'd caught the flu and been bed-bound for two days straight.

But he'd also never had such a chance to be famous.

'I can't do Saturday,' Zak replied urgently. 'I've got a big match in the cup. Can we do another day? Saturday afternoon even?'

Tony sighed audibly. Zak could picture him on the other end of the phone line, hands on his face, eyes screwed up, teeth sparkling. 'No can do. When you've got as many followers as Baller B you don't get much spare time. He's got other social media stars to film with. He's got advertisements to film. There's an autobiography he's writing. Meetings with television executives. Time in the recording studio to work on his new music track – and that's all happening just this week. You're going to have to be a little flexible here.'

All Zak was asking for was one afternoon. 'How about next

week, then?' Zak asked with increasing desperation. He could feel his hand becoming clammy, his heart pounding. What would Chloe say to him missing the game, so soon after missing the concert with her? How would Mr Jones react? What if they lost the game because he wasn't there?

'Zak, Zak, Zak,' Tony laughed. Zak couldn't help but notice that Tony was no longer calling him by the nickname that he hadn't agreed to. He couldn't help but notice that Tony's laugh wasn't so much of a laugh as a sneer. 'The online world moves quickly. Today's viral video is yesterday's ice bucket challenge. We need to move quickly because, let's be blunt, you're still not well known. Surely you saw that at the shopping centre? But you will be soon. There's still hype around you. People are hungry for content from @therealTekkerZak. They need that as quickly as possible or they'll become bored and find the latest hot new talent to watch instead.'

'But we could record my skills from the game and use that as my new video?' Zak suggested weakly. 'I've been working on some dope stuff with Chloe. I know it'll look sick on camera.'

'Zak, we don't want you to become a one-trick pony. You've already done that. It worked well, but your followers don't want to see the same video. They want to see you with talents like Baller B, not with your teammates at Redwood.'

Zak knew he was fighting a losing battle. He took a deep breath, letting the air flow into his lungs. Upstairs he could hear his dad pottering about. He'd been thrilled when Zak had told him there was a chance he'd be filming with Baller B. They both knew it was quick progress. The video, the agent, the social media stars: everything was falling into place. He couldn't disrupt that. Better to miss one game than to miss an opportunity like this.

'Zak, are you still there?' he heard his *enabler*'s voice on the other end of the line. Another deep breath. He had to say it.

'Yes.'

'Yes you're there?'

'Yes, I'm here. I'll do it.'

He'd only miss one game. It wasn't the end of the world.

YouTube subscribers: 36,304
Instagram followers: 23,123
Twitter followers: 3,984

'You're doing what?'

Zak couldn't see Mr Jones, but he could picture him at the other end of the phone line, scratching his head in confusion. 'You can't play because you're shooting a video, did you say?'

'Yes,' Zak replied.

'What kind of video?'

'For YouTube. My agent has sorted it all out. It's a collaboration with Baller B. He's a really famous YouTuber.'

Mr Jones emitted a sigh of exasperation.

'And there's no other time you can do this?'

'No. I tried, honest, I did. Baller B is so busy though that Saturday is the only time he can shoot the video.'

'Son, I want what's best for you and I'm going to be honest,

I'm not sure this video lark is. You've got serious talent on the football pitch. It'd be a shame to see it go to waste.'

'But it's only one game!' Zak objected. 'I'll be back for the one after.'

'That's what they all say,' Mr Jones replied. 'But when you start putting stuff before your football, it becomes less of a priority. Suddenly football seems less important. You've already missed one game, so what if you miss another?'

'That won't happen,' Zak promised. But even as the words came out, he knew it was a promise he couldn't keep. Everything now depended on Tony. If Tony said he couldn't play then he couldn't play and that was final.

Mr Jones was silent for a few seconds.

'Make sure you're at training next week, Oxden. I'll allow this as a one-off and I mean it.'

Zak breathed a sigh of relief. Mr Jones disapproved, that much was clear. He could hear it in the pronounced tone of his voice, the fact that he called him by his surname rather than his first name. But at least he was going to allow it as a one-off. In Zak's book, that meant that Mr Jones was convinced. Next came the real challenge: Chloe.

He couldn't just call her like he had Mr Jones. No matter what had happened between them recently, she was his best mate. She deserved to be told properly, not fobbed off. But as he turned onto Glenn Close the perfectly symmetrical trees didn't seem reassuring. They were intimidating, towering over him. The houses were too big. The road too perfect. Was it too late to go back to his house? With every step, he wished he had just phoned Chloe. She was going to react badly whatever.

A wave of guilt swept over him as he remembered cancelling on her to go to the shopping centre. He disappointed her and was only left disappointed himself. He pictured a scene where he was in the crowd watching Peakz with his best mate, rapping along to the beat. For a moment he felt regret. No, he couldn't feel regret. He had to shake himself out of this. He was a star now and had to act like a star, just like Tony told him to. Superstars had no regrets. They made their decisions and acted on them. They were strong and sure of themselves. Just like he had to be.

Mrs Smith opened the door and answered with a smile as soon as she saw Zak, just as she always did.

'Hiya, Zak. Ever so good to see you. You must have smelt my blueberry muffins.' She giggled to herself as the smell of home baking wafted through from the kitchen. His mouth began to water just as his cheeks went red.

'Hi, Mrs Smith. Good to see you too. Is Chloe in?'

'I'll just check. Chloe!' Mrs Smith turned and called up the stairs.

'Who is it?' Chloe's voice drifted down from the direction of the bedroom.

'It's Zak,' he chimed in before Mrs Smith had the chance.

Thirty seconds later Chloe was standing in front of him and Mrs Smith had rushed off to get biscuits and drinks.

'Yeah?' Chloe's voice was wooden.

'Fancy a kickabout?' Zak asked. He knew his best way to break the news to Chloe was to get back in her good books.

'Where were you today?'

'I wasn't feeling great this morning. I'm better now though.'

he smiled at her to prove his health. 'So how about that kickabout?'

'You've not got a video to shoot instead?' Chloe sneered.

'No, come on.' Zak realised he was already fighting a losing battle. 'Let's go and do bits in the garden. Bit of weak foot training?'

'You're not going to film it, are you?'

'What?' Zak acted surprised. 'I'm doing it because I want to improve.'

'Don't you have somewhere better to be?' Chloe sniffed at him.

'Not that I know of,' he shrugged.

'Won't *your fans* miss you?'

'I'm sure the five who bothered to watch me at the shopping centre won't mind.'

'Fine. Let's go.'

Chloe worked at a frantic speed. Mr Jones had always told them that the best way to practise was at 'match speed'. She tore around the garden, moving the ball around as if it were glued to her foot. Zak watched, catching his breath while she worked to make her weakness into a strength.

After forty-five minutes of training in silence they retired to the welcoming sight of Mrs Smith's muffins and drinks.

'So how was Peakz?' Zak asked.

'Chris fainted with excitement,' Chloe said in her matter-of-fact tone. 'I might as well have gone on my own.' Zak chuckled at the thought.

'Yeah, but how was Peakz?'

'Sick.'

'I bet he was.'

'And what about your amazing show for your fans?'

'I got detention for looking at my phone, had no time to prepare, messed up my routine, fell over, disappointed the people watching and only had five people watching anyway.' That seemed to cheer Chloe up. Sensing the tide turning, Zak pointed to the Xbox. 'Best of three?' he suggested. Chloe couldn't help but smile. He could tell that their session in the garden had at least put her in a better mood, and he knew she could never turn down an opportunity to beat him at *FIFA*.

Her mood soon improved further.

'What are you doing?' Zak screamed. 'We're playing gentlemen's rules.'

He'd accidentally pressed the A button, making his goalkeeper pass the ball straight to Chloe's waiting striker.

'Well guess what?' Chloe laughed. 'I'm no gentleman.' She shot into the empty goal before directing her player to wheel off in celebration while Zak raged on the sofa.

He never got close to making a comeback. Chloe won all three games.

'What do you reckon about the game this weekend then?' Chloe said as Zak made to leave.

His heart froze. The game. He'd forgotten about telling her.

'Erm, well,' he mumbled. 'You see. The thing is, Chloe, I can't play in . . .'

'What?'

'I can't play in the game this Saturday.'

'Why?' Chloe's whole demeanour changed in an instant. From the warm, funny character who took pride in beating

Zak she flicked like a switch. There was nothing warm about the girl who had been made to stop in her tracks by Zak. Her arms were folded, her lips pursed.

'Tony is making me shoot a video. I tried to get out of it, I swear.' It was hopeless. Chloe would never buy that.

'Yeah, sure. I bet you begged Tony to let you play.' Her words dripped with sarcasm.

'I did. Honestly. But it's with Baller B. You know him? He's massive on social media.' Zak was begging now. The words tumbled from his mouth, trying to show Chloe just why he had no option but to shoot the video.

'Whatever,' Chloe replied. 'You go shoot your video. We'll be fine without you.'

YouTube subscribers: 42,873
Instagram followers: 25,674
Twitter followers: 4,851

'Zed Dog, good to see you my man.' Tony held out his fist for Zak to bump.

'Hello, Mr Curtis!' Zak's dad followed behind. He decided to shake Tony by the hand rather than fist-bump him. 'Fine day for it, eh?' he added, looking around at the park.

'Glorious,' Tony commented. 'Baller B's over on the basketball court. There's two goals there so that's where we'll do the first section of filming.'

Baller B wasn't as Zak expected. Sure, there was the messy blond hair and the black hoodie and even a snapback emblazoned with B, the logo of his own merchandise. But then there was his personality. In the videos online he was full of personality, oozing confidence and always willing to joke about. In person he was the opposite. It was as if he led two lives.

Zak moved forward and held out his fist when Tony introduced him. 'Nice to meet you,' he said.

Baller B didn't look up from his phone. His thumb swiped frantically at the screen. With his free hand he held up his first. Taking the cue, Zak extended his first forward and bumped it against the pale skin of Baller B.

'It's a pleasure to meet you.' Zak's dad stepped out from behind and shook Baller B's fist. Baller B looked up in surprise. His eyes flitted upward in a quick, jerky movement. They briefly appraised Zak's dad, and then returned straight back to his phone, his thumb continuing to swipe.

Zak gave his dad a nervous glance. How were they going to make an engaging video with this guy?

While Tony discussed the best shooting angles with Nat and Zak's dad ran between locations on the court to place cones, Zak did his best to spark Baller B into conversation. Yet with every question, Baller B cut him off with single-word answers or merely ignored him.

'Those *FIFA* videos you make, they're amazing!' Zak tried.

'Yeah,' Baller B replied, still looking at his phone.

'And that *FIFA* celebrations skit was too much.'

'For sure.'

'I've just started making football freestyle videos, you know. It's all about tekkers.'

'Cool.'

'I reckon our video is going to be lit.'

'Yeah.'

'Filming with you is going to give me some serious clout.'

'Cool.'

That moment Tony rescued Zak by shouting the pair over to the centre of the court and Zak couldn't help but feel relieved. He'd have had a better conversation with the back of his own hand. Still, if Baller B could help raise his profile then Zak didn't mind having hundreds of awkward conversations with him.

Tony told them that they were going to start by filming a skills video. A simple crossbar challenge followed by five attempts at getting the ball through the basketball hoop with their feet. Tony wanted plenty of energy and plenty of banter between the pair.

As soon as the cameras started rolling, Baller B jumped into life. It was as if the power of the lens flipped a switch inside him. Gone was the monotone teenager, replaced by a dazzling, energetic YouTuber. 'Yo I'm Baller B!' he bounced around the basketball court, his hands a flurry of activity. 'And this guy here,' the camera panned to Zak. He was freestyling in the background, pulling off consecutive around the worlds. 'This is Zak. You might know him as TekkerZak and if you don't then why don't you! Click follow right now. Anyway, he's called TekkerZak because he reckons he's got some tekkers. So let's see if it's true.'

That was the first segment filmed. Zak was buzzing. The skills, though only in the background, had been executed to perfection. 'Hey, what's that?' Baller B pointed down at Zak's shirt. Zak looked at the finger, only for Baller B to raise his hand and slap Zak's chin. It was the oldest trick in the book and Baller B burst into uncontrollable laughter. 'Yes!' he yelled into the camera. 'It never fails! 1-0 to me.'

Where was this energy earlier? Perhaps Baller B had just been shy? If that was the case, his behaviour had changed wildly. Confidence oozed from him. Zak was determined now, driven not just to show his skills, but to beat Baller B. In his five attempts, he hit the crossbar three times. He didn't celebrate, turning to the camera and acting like it was normal for him to hit the crossbar – even though inside his body was roaring with happiness. Baller B, in contrast, hit the crossbar just once and celebrated as if he'd just won the World Cup. Nat desperately chased after him as he did a lap of the basketball court, waving his hoodie over his head and then tossing his personalised snapback into the camera lens.

Then it was onto the basketball hoop. Zak hit his first attempt right through the hoop. Sensing he was in trouble, Baller B sabotaged Zak's next effort, kicking his ball at Zak just as Zak's foot hit his own ball. Instead of heading toward the hoop, his effort veered off wildly. For a microsecond he was angry, but then he remembered the cameras. Everything he did had to be decided by them now. His actions were no longer dictated by his feelings but by the lenses that surrounded him. What could he do to go viral? Zak took a step forward and stumbled on purpose, then fell. He could picture it now, millions of people all around the world laughing and saying 'no way!'

Things had been ramped up.

Zak didn't mind making a fool of himself if he could also dazzle with his skills. For his next attempt he put his headband over his eyes and threw in some groundmoves before lifting the ball carefully into the hoop. As the ball thunked against the backboard and then swished through the net, Zak strolled over to Baller B, aware of all of the cameras following him. 'Game over,' he smiled, removing Baller B's snapback and putting it on his own head. Baller B, he was pleased to see, stood open-mouthed. There was no way he was beating that.

YouTube subscribers: 177,327
Instagram followers: 105,898
Twitter followers: 30,067

Zak had recently begun to think of himself as fairly famous. People knew him and followers waited for his next piece of content with their notifications switched on. But now Zak knew that he hadn't really been famous. Not *that* famous. Because after the video with Baller B, everything went to a new level of crazy.

Missing the match had been the best decision of his life.

He didn't even care how Redwood had done. Suddenly the county cup seemed insignificant. It was only when he read Cynthia Johnson's report in that Monday's *Redwood Review* that he found out his team had toiled to a close victory on penalties after drawing 0-0 in normal time. The best possible result, Zak reflected. Redwood won, but had obviously missed his presence. Why else would they have failed to score?

Zak's face now seemed to be everywhere. His follower numbers trebled. Someone created a fan account for him. The new hashtag that Tony had told him to use to promote the video, #KeepItTekk, was trending. Influencers were posting reaction videos. Most importantly, the video with Baller B had been viewed seven million times.

Seven million.

Every time he whispered that number it seemed unreal. A number that big – more than 10% of the entire population of the UK – all for him.

This was too much. Surely this couldn't be happening. How had that very first video, the one filmed on a whim in his back garden, turned into all this? Zak just couldn't believe it.

Tony called it The Snowball. 'You've been running up the mountain all this time, Zed Dog,' he told Zak on the phone. 'This is what you've been waiting for. The Snowball has come along and now you're rolling down that mountain, getting bigger and bigger with each video. Seven million views. Let's keep rolling with The Snowball. Let's roll with it as hard as we can for as long as we can. By the end, we'll be getting seventy million views on each video. We just need to keep on rolling.'

All Zak could do was to trust Tony. After all, it had been Tony who had got all of his other clients to give a shoutout for Zak and Baller B's video. It had been Tony who had suggested the hashtag. It had been Tony who told him the precise time to upload the video so that the majority of his followers would see it (5pm, so that he was hitting the west coast of America as they woke up and Asia as they went to bed).

Tony knew all of the tricks of the trade.

'Engagement, engagement, engagement,' he told Zak. 'Engage with your fans as much as you can.'

Tony's formula was simple. Engagement meant comments. Comments meant more views. More views meant more likes. More likes meant more engagement. Simple tricks like spelling the name of the video wrong increased engagement. 'Tekkers wiht Baller B' led to hundreds of comments telling Zak that you don't spell 'with' as 'wiht'. The comments soon spiralled out of control. Zak just didn't have the time to reply to every single one, so his dad took charge, liking any comments with #instasquad or #KeepItTekk and replying to anything from his most fanatical followers. The formula repeated itself, and the more it repeated itself, the more money there was to be made. And now they really were making money. The money from YouTube had trickled in at first, but now it poured in. A thousand pounds here, ten thousand pounds there. *Ten thousand pounds.* The figure made him go weak at the knees. How could anyone ever be given that much money at once? And just for shooting a video! Not that Zak ever saw much of the money. His dad looked after the money. It went toward the house, making sure his dad didn't have to worry about getting work, and the rest was put in to a trust that he'd be able to access when he was older. The thought astounded him. A 13-year-old kid, making tens of thousands of pounds each month. While all of his mates were playing *FIFA* and kicking about in the park, he was earning money.

That's the problem with money. Earning becomes addictive. There's always more to earn. It becomes a competition.

And he had a competition to win.

To do so he had to keep riding The Snowball.

He had to build on the buzz and release his next video as soon as he could.

With his new ambition, everything became about filming. There wasn't time for anything else. He filmed for three days straight, missing school on each of the days in order to get a full day of filming. That suited Zak. What good would the Industrial Revolution do for his videos? His dad was less sure, but Tony convinced him it'd only be a short-term measure. Just while The Snowball was rolling. He filmed more skills videos, started a series of skills tutorial videos, streamed himself playing *FIFA*, joined Baller B for Instagram Live sessions. His whole life was captured on camera then repackaged for social media.

Zak barely even had time to check the messages on his phone during those long, energy-sapping days. That was now his dad's task, just like Tony had said it would be. Since signing with Tony his dad hadn't needed to worry about working a single day on site. Now, it seemed, Zak was his job. That's why he was able to dedicate so much time to his son. Keeping track of Zak's phone was easy for him to do. If Tony phoned then Zak's dad would pick it up. That was it.

The messages on the Redwood Legends WhatsApp group went unanswered. His friends could wait. School could wait. Redwood Rovers could wait. Chloe could wait. The Snowball couldn't.

YouTube subscribers: 202,419
Instagram followers: 60,433
Twitter followers: 40,421

Amongst the brick buildings and swirling litterbins and loud teachers of Redwood Community College, Zak could sense a change. Not in the day to day movements of the school, because like every day, they remained the same. Still, Mrs Turnbull prowled outside the front gates, shouting at pupils to meet the uniform rules. Still, he walked the stuffy corridors with his friends. Still, the bell dinged every day at exactly the same minute of exactly the same hour. But though everything was the same, everything was also different. It had been just under a week since he'd last walked these corridors. At the start of the school year he had been Zak. Then he became @therealTekkerZak. But now he was @therealTekkerZak, collaborator with Baller B and creator of videos that were watched *millions* of times. He wasn't like any of the other pupils in the school.

In lessons he sat quietly and did as he was told, all the while desperately trying to fight the urge to check his phone and refresh his following. It proved hard to concentrate. He'd only missed a few days and yet already he felt further behind than his classmates. At breaktime and lunchtime he joined in with the tennis ball matches on the playground and did his best to impress and laugh along with his friends. The warmth his closest friends had previously shown had notably cooled. They remained impressed by his achievements but were no longer so vocal. Maybe it was because he missed the county cup game. Perhaps it was because he hadn't replied to their messages. Well, Tony had told him he'd have to make sacrifices . . . As the bell went he couldn't wait to rush home. He didn't want to be trapped in school like everyone else, confined to the same rules and times as the 1,000 others who wore the same clothes and ate the same cheap canteen food.

When the final bell went to signal the day's end, he found himself alone. Chloe had blanked him for the whole day and hadn't waited for him to bike home. There was no sign of her. Zak didn't mind. She'd only moan at him about the match anyway. He wanted to go home alone and spend the evening speaking to his fans and dreaming up new videos. He followed the long corridor of the main building out toward the science department and then along the walkway to the open bike cage.

That's when he saw them.

After the first incident they'd stayed away, content that they'd scared him. Zak had seen them since, but they'd never bothered to approach him again. Until now. They strolled toward him slowly yet purposefully, spreading out into a circle so that Zak had nowhere to run. He was trapped.

'Well, well, well,' the ringleader said menacingly. 'Big man just got even bigger, didn't he?'

'What do you want?' Zak's voice squeaked. He sounded even younger than a 13-year-old. He had never been more aware of his age or his size. The ringleader laughed and his laughter was echoed by the other two.

'We haven't seen you around recently. We just wanted to check up on how you're doing.' Zak knew that wasn't true. The ringleader was using a sickly-sweet voice.

'I'm fine. Can I go now?' Zak took two quick steps forward but found his path blocked.

'Ooh, he's in a rush,' the one with long brown hair chirped. 'He's too important to talk to us. Out of his way, fellas.'

'Yes, best get out of the way for the superstar,' the third one chimed in, his hoodie pulled tight over his head. Zak could taste the salt in his sweat. Every one of his senses was running riot. He knew he was in danger.

'Okay, we'll get out of the way,' the ringleader said. 'But first, we might as well give him something to remember us, what do you say?' His friends nodded their heads in unison. The ringleader smiled, flashing his pointed teeth. And then Zak was on the floor. His world went sideways as the force of the punch knocked him clean off his feet. It came so quickly that he hadn't even seen it. The right side of his face pulsated angrily from the ringleader's knuckles. Zak opened his mouth to scream out in pain but no sound came. Blood dripped onto the concrete, and then tears. Distantly, he heard them walking away. He was alone now, he knew that. With all of his effort, he propped his head upward and spat out another mouthful of blood. Two of his teeth had been loosened and wobbled in his mouth. He had to breathe deeply, to focus himself once more. Circles clouded his vision, chasing each other around his eyes. How had that just happened? Why had that just happened?

His dad was washing up a particularly dirty saucepan when Zak opened the front door. Tony sat on the sofa, talking confidently into his mobile phone. Together, they cried out in horror. The saucepan crashed to the floor and wobbled until it lay forgotten.

'What the hell has happened to you?' his dad asked, rushing over to him.

'It was nothing.' Zak brushed him off, eager to shut himself in his room. Tony's phone sat against his upraised palm but he wasn't saying anything. For once in his life, Tony had been left speechless.

'There's blood all down you,' his dad said. 'That's not nothing!' He hugged Zak in close and Zak could brush him away no more. Before he could stop them, tears rolled down his cheeks. His dad's touch was so reassuring, so caring.

'I'll call you back,' Tony muttered in the background.

It could have been minutes, it could have been hours, but eventually Zak felt ready to talk. He told his dad and Tony about the three year 11s and their threats, then their punch. His dad was horrified, Tony was outraged.

'You can't go back there,' Tony announced. 'I've been saying it to your dad for some time but this is the final straw.' His dad just stared blankly, still unable to comprehend what had happened. 'Ever since they kept you in detention and made you mess up that routine. That's the problem with schools. They aren't aspirational enough. Why does Zak need an education to fall back on in case he doesn't make it as a social media star? Of course he's going to make it. Anyone who says otherwise is just negative. And why does he need to spend all day with other kids? He should be hanging around with other YouTubers.'

Zak didn't want to go back. He never wanted to be in a situation where he could feel so threatened again. He wanted the safety of his videos, to interact with the followers who gave him such thrills.

'Mr Curtis, I'm not so sure,' his dad replied. 'We shouldn't overreact.'

'Overreact!' Tony screamed. 'Overreact? Look at his face. It looks like a dog's dinner.' Zak hadn't yet looked in the mirror and nor did he want to. 'He's going to have a black eye and a cut all down his face.'

'I'll speak to the school and book a meeting with Mr Davies.'

'I'd already told Mr Davies about them,' Zak responded limply. 'He did nothing.'

'And I tell you why we need to pull him out of school!' Tony was on a roll now, his angry words sparking angrier words. Nobody got in Tony Curtis's way. 'Appearance matters in this industry. Who's going to want to hire Zak if he's got a black eye or cuts and bruises up his face?'

'But what about his friends? His education?' His dad had never stood up to Tony before. He'd always seemed in awe of him, swept up in every suggestion he made. Why did he have to disagree now?

'I'll still see them at Redwood Rovers!' Zak butted in. He was firmly on Tony's side. 'And I can learn at home. Loads of kids are home-schooled. What about that time when all the schools closed because of the virus? You taught me then, didn't you?' Tony shoved his hands onto his hips and raised himself onto the balls of his feet. He stared at Zak's dad, daring him to say something. Zak's dad looked at Zak, really looked at him. There was love in his eyes. Zak was all he had.

'I'm not sure—' he started.

'Fine. I didn't want to have to say this yet but I'm left with no choice. Listen, The Snowball has been good to us and as far as I'm concerned it's time to cash in. That person I was just speaking to on the phone was from a megabrand. I'm talking one of the biggest in the world. They make the football boots you wear, in fact. Well, you won't have to buy those boots anymore. After seeing your video with Baller B, Panther Sports wants to be your sponsor.' Zak felt as if he'd been hit all over again. But this time there was no pain, only joy. Panther Sports! His sponsor! 'But they won't want you to be in their adverts if you look like that,' Tony sneered. 'So here's what's going to happen. Zak will stay out of school. Listen to me, Dean,' he raised his finger as Zak's dad began to speak. 'I'm only talking short term. For the next few weeks until we know it's safe for him to return. We can't risk this sponsorship because of a school scuffle. They're willing to pay £100,000 to Zak for wearing their boots and promoting their brand. Let me repeat that, *£100,000*. Promise me you'll take him out of school for a few weeks and then I'll call Panther Sports back and tell them we've got a deal.'

'Please, Dad. Please,' Zak begged. Free football boots! Panther Sports as his sponsor! And then there was the money, but most of all the free football boots! The Snowball truly had been good. This was exhilarating, his whole body was electrified.

His dad knew he had no choice. Who in their right mind would turn down £100,000? 'Fine,' he replied. 'But just for a few weeks.'

27

YouTube subscribers: 227,053
Instagram followers: 138,349
Twitter followers: 49,046

One week became two. Then three. Then four. The contract with Panther Sports came through and it was beyond Zak's wildest dreams. £100,000 just for wearing all of the free kit and boots Panther Sports sent him in his own videos and for appearing in five adverts for them in the next year. Truth be told, he'd have appeared in the adverts for free.

Without school, his life had become one of constant routine. He woke at the same time every day, practised at the same time every day and went to bed at the same time every day.

Film. Upload. Film. Upload. With Tony handling his business, his dad dealing with his comments and messages, Nat filming and Jazz creating amazing video content, Zak needed to focus on little else.

The only time he ever broke from the routine was to go to Redwood Rovers' training – and only then if he'd finished all of the filming that had been planned. Just like he had felt at school, however, everything was different. The teammates who had previously bigged up his skills and been in awe of his videos were still impressed, but their interest too had cooled. Gone were the requests for selfies and video shoutouts, replaced by teammates equally in awe of him and distant to him, as if his celebrity was normal but he was not. Zak laughed along with them, did his best to join in with their jokes, but at the same time he too couldn't help feeling that something had changed between them. It was like he didn't belong with them anymore. Did he have anything in common? Not school. Not normal life. What did talking about school and what they watched on Netflix the night before matter to him?

If he was going to make it as a star, he had to sacrifice everything.

Playing and training as a footballer was still beautiful, the purest form of enjoyment that Zak enjoyed. But there was no immediate impact. When he posted a video the likes and follows came instantly. So did the money. But when he played for Redwood, three points didn't mean anything until the league was over. A good training session would only have impact in the years to come, not instantly. And so when he had to choose between training and filming, the decision was easy.

Chloe grew more distant. On the pitch she did what was needed. She passed to him if he was in a better position, brought her marker short so Zak could run into the space created, but off the pitch she avoided him.

It all frustrated Mr Jones, who told Zak every time he saw him that he needed more discipline if he was going to become a professional footballer. 'You're wasting your talent,' he said. 'Don't regret wasting it for a few likes on the internet.'

Zak nodded at Mr Jones and smiled, but he knew that the man didn't understand. He could never understand. They didn't even have social media when Mr Jones was a teenager! What could Mr Jones possibly know about YouTube and all of the amazing opportunities it could unlock?

And soon enough, the most amazing of opportunities came Zak's way. Panther Sports wanted to fly him out to Barcelona to star in an advert alongside Cristiano Ronaldo, Ronaldinho and Jadon Sancho. On top of that, they'd put him up in a seven-star hotel overlooking the Barceloneta beach and throw in VIP tickets to the El Clasico game between Barcelona and Real Madrid on one condition: Zak freestyled on the hallowed Camp Nou surface at half-time in the match.

Even Mr Jones had to admit that was pretty cool.

Zak felt like he was flying. It was as if his soul had been lifted from his body and was soaring in celebration. The Camp Nou! Freestyling with the legends whose posters lined his bedroom walls!

For the first time in a long time, he unlocked his phone not to communicate with his followers, but with his friends.

REDWOOD LEGENDS
Zak: Youll nevr guess what!! Im gonna go to Barcelona and film wiv CR7 R10 and Jadon Sancho! Plus I get tickets to el clasico. Maddddddd!

Chris: 😮
Marcus: get CR7s number for me
Josh: Thats wicked man
Chloe: Nice one

For the first time in a long time, he couldn't wait to see them in person. That evening Zak walked in to Redwood Rovers' training session feeling ten feet tall. His friends crowded him when he arrived, patting him on the back and fist-bumping him in congratulations. The confidence flowed onto the pitch, where he gave a masterclass in close ball control and deadly finishing. Nobody could get near him. When the session ended, Zak reflected on a brilliant day. With the confidence still running high, he decided to patch up one final thing: his relationship with Chloe.

'Chloe!' he called out to her as she walked toward the car park. She must have heard him – he shouted so loudly that she couldn't possibly have missed it – but she carried on walking. Zak chased after her, reaching her just before the dimly lit car park.

'Chloe, what's up, how's it going?'

Chloe slowed and looked into the distance. 'Fine,' she said flatly. 'Not as well as it's going for you, it seems.'

'Yeah, I know, I'm buzzing. But how are you? It's been ages.'

'That's nothing to do with me. I'm always about for you. I just wish it was the same with you.'

'I do too, Chloe, swear down. It's just Tony . . .'

'Yeah, yeah – Tony, Tony, Tony,' Chloe cut him off. 'When did we last play *FIFA* or go for a kickabout? What about the

Peakz concert? I don't even know why you aren't at school anymore. We're supposed to be best mates.'

'Look, I want to hang out, but it's hard right now. Tony's making me do so much and I have to keep filming. Need to make it. You know the vibe.'

Chloe sighed and started walking again. 'No, Zak, I don't know the vibe. I don't know anything about you anymore. You've changed.'

'I haven't!' Zak protested.

'Why don't you message us anymore then? Not just me, but your other friends. You don't see us in school, you don't speak to us outside of school and you run off as soon as training is over. You haven't been to knock for me once. It's a joke. I know you have to make sacrifices to succeed, but why sacrifice friends for followers? Your followers don't care about you. They won't help you in the bad times. Neither will Tony. And if you keep going, you won't have any friends to help you when you need them.'

'Chloe, you're my best mate,' Zak pleaded.

'What's the point of being mates if you don't even make the time to see me?'

'I can. I will. Listen, when I get back from Barcelona we'll go for a kickabout.'

Chloe laughed. But it wasn't a warm laugh. It was hollow. 'But we won't, will we? Because there'll be another video for you to film. You can't just disconnect from real life, Zak. You can't spend all of your time in the digital world.'

'And you can't ignore the digital world, Chloe.' Zak could feel his own frustration beginning to bubble up inside him.

Could she never be pleased for him? Yes, he'd been absent but he'd been busy. This was his success. He'd hoped she'd share in it. 'Look at the opportunities it's giving me. Look at the people who watch my content.'

'It won't last forever. In a few months something else will come along and everyone will start watching that instead.'

'You're wrong!' Zak shouted. He couldn't help it. Chloe had hit a nerve. The bubbles of frustration became steam, then fire that he had to unleash. 'They call me an influencer. You know why? Because I influence people. I'll carry on influencing people. What do you do? Nothing. Nobody even knows you exist!'

Everything stopped. Silence swept through the trees and across the park. Zak stood there in the semi-darkness, breathing heavily in his anger as Chloe absorbed his words. She gulped, and for a second her entire body tensed up, then she blinked and she was back, as composed as ever.

'Goodbye, Zak,' Chloe replied.

With that, she walked away from him and into her parents' waiting car.

Zak didn't know when he'd see her again.

And what's more, he realised he didn't much care.

YouTube subscribers: 399,953
Instagram followers: 256,304
Twitter followers: 68,046

If life was a video game then Zak had completed it. That was all he could think of as he stepped onto the private jet that Panther Sports had commissioned exclusively to fly him out to Barcelona. No more flights in economy with heated-up plastic food for £9.99 and screaming babies and knees cramped into the reclined seat in front. The private plane was so big that Zak could have run laps of it. There were beds and games consoles and televisions with all of the latest films and even a pool table. 'Coca-Cola, sir?' His own personal waiter stood in the aisle, willing to wait on him hand and foot throughout the two-hour flight. 'Please,' Zak replied with a nod.

At the other end, a Rolls-Royce Phantom waited for him. As soon as the plane touched down he was whisked off with his dad and Tony and placed in the back of the car that was the same size as Zak's bedroom on King's Lane. The chauffeur had specific instructions to drop them at their hotel – the most luxurious on Barcelona's beach front – and then take them to the Royal Yacht Club. The sea glistened through the tinted windows as they were driven north along the coastline to the city. Barcelona's ancient buildings and unique architecture dotted the skyline up ahead. The city soon swallowed them up. The open road became high rise apartments, then the stone buildings and Gaudi-inspired designs of the Gothic Quarter. Just before the famous Sagrada Familia, they turned right, back towards the coastline. Zak couldn't stop staring. There was something of interest in every direction. Tourists clicking their cameras. Buildings built more than a thousand years before. Streets dug out where they had no right to be, meandering between nooks and crannies to transport people around the city. Restaurants spilling out onto the streets and roads, their tables full of diners eating paella and tapas. Even through the closed windows, the noise was deafening.

The hotel was everything it promised to be and more. Zak and his dad had been booked into a room on the 23rd floor. But not just any room: the executive suite with its own jacuzzi, series of widescreen televisions and welcoming fruit bowls. 'This is how you know this place is good,' his dad said when he found that the room also included a trouser press machine. 'Yes, this is the good life.'

Despite being less than 500 metres from the hotel, the chauffeur insisted on driving them to the Royal Yacht Club. He had clear instructions. Waiting in the marina was Ebony, the head of talent for Panther Sports. She greeted Tony like an old friend and then made a fuss over Zak and his dad. Everything was happening so fast. 'They're all here,' she said breezily. 'Come and see them.' A light breeze ruffled Zak's hair as he followed Ebony down the planks of the marina. The sun, shining down on them, was a perfect circle. Seagulls squawked above. If they were going to be fed, they wanted to eat the finest food that Barcelona had to offer. Ebony turned at the furthest mooring station and suddenly they were in the shade. Zak looked up to see the sun blocked in the sky by the tallest, grandest, most luxurious boat he'd ever seen. Even in the movies they weren't this big. 'Hey!' a voice came from the deck. Zak looked up and almost fell back into the clear seawater. It was Cristiano Ronaldo, his top off and a drink in his hand. 'Come on up,' he offered.

Zak's nerves jangled as he got closer to the man he'd spent countless hours pretending to be down at the park with Chloe. Together they'd tried to copy his unique dipping free-kicks. They'd jumped backwards just like he did when he scored and roared 'Siiii!', just like him. You never expect to meet your heroes. His legs felt faint. The steps up to the yacht seemed so steep. Suddenly the length of the journey hit him and he felt tired. His emotions were all over the place. There he was, just in front of Zak, smiling his trademark smile. His body was perfectly sculpted. The muscles shouted out at Zak. It was no mistake that he was one of the best players ever. He'd had to work relentlessly for every single achievement. 'You must be TekkerZak,' Ronaldo said. 'I've heard a lot about you.'

That really was too much. Zak didn't know what to do. He was so shocked that he was rooted to the spot, like a scarecrow on a fine summer day. He opened his mouth and nothing came out. Ronaldo laughed a friendly laugh. 'Hey, R10, come and meet TekkerZak.' A straggly haired Brazilian poked his head out of a window on the upper deck. It really was him. 'Yo,' he said, sticking out his thumb and pinky and waving them at Zak in the traditional Brazilian manner. Zak raised his hand to wave back, all of the time wondering if this was really happening. That morning he'd been in Redwood. And now he was here, on a luxury yacht in Barcelona with two of his idols.

Ronaldinho sauntered down from the upper deck with a football in his hands. 'Freestyle, bro?' he asked Zak. Stunned, Zak nodded his head. The Brazilian tossed Zak the ball and he caught it on his foot. As the ball settled, he wondered what else he could possibly achieve in life. How could he ever top this moment?

There was one way, actually. He turned to see Tony holding his iPhone out and felt a huge sigh of relief. Every touch was being recorded. He'd be able to share it on his social media channels later. Now there really was no chance he could ever top the moment.

The next day Zak found himself on set with his idols, surrounded by cameras of all shapes and sizes. They were shooting the advert at Barcelona's famous academy, La Masia. The new Panther Sports range was all about freedom, they were told. Wearing their kit helped players to play with freedom, and so the advert would show various players playing with freedom. Though Zak's segment was small – just a couple of seconds of skills – it still took several hours to film. Laden in the latest Panther Sports kit, he had to pretend to stop dead in the middle of a football game and start freestyling. As Zak waited around for the first take, he knew he had to put all of his effort into impressing his idols with his skills. The cameras didn't matter to him. They were normal now. His whole life was filmed on camera, after all. But performing in front of his idols…it was enough to make his nerves jangle. The cameras rolled and he dropped the ball and fumbled his transitions, but he also succeeded in pulling off some of his sickest tricks in other takes. By the end of the morning, he'd given the cameras more than enough content for his part of the advert. The camera crew all told him they were impressed and that he was fantastic. His idols congratulated him and told him he was great and fist-bumped him, but Zak couldn't help but notice that they all seemed so much surer of themselves when they were filmed pulling off their own skills. They weren't even freestylers. They were footballers first, freestylers second. And yet their skills were even better than Zak's. The muscles that rippled through Cristiano Ronaldo's vest weren't a mistake. Nor was Ronaldinho's smoothness or Jadon Sancho's electric feet. They were all the product of hard work. If Zak was going to reach their elite level and become one of the world's best freestylers, he'd have to work just as hard as they had. No, even harder.

'Look who it is!' Zak's dad whispered in his ear as they waited for Jadon Sancho to finish his segment. The FC Barcelona first team had finished their morning training session and much of the squad was now lingering at the side of the pitch. 'Hey, TekkerZak,' Ronaldo shouted. He was standing in the middle of the players. 'Come meet everyone.' Zak wandered over in a daze. Stars filled his vision. Ronaldo put his arm around him.

Zak winced as he felt the contact. This was actually happening. 'This is my friend, TekkerZak. He's got very good skills.' My *friend*. He'd actually said my friend!

That evening, they were all invited to Ronaldinho's luxury restaurant in the exclusive area of Eixample. Zak exchanged numbers with all of his idols, promised to keep in touch, was followed back by all of them on social media. How could this be real? Any moment now, he'd surely wake up. A smile crossed his face as he thought of how his Redwood mates would react if they could see him now. Chris would be left speechless. Marcus might faint. Josh would be taking as many selfies as physically possible. And then there was Chloe. She'd be grilling Ronaldinho on his training routine. He imagined her next to him, smiling in her white Nikes, ball tucked under her arm. But then he remembered what had happened the last time he saw Chloe. No, he couldn't let bad thoughts enter his mind. This was epic. This was everything.

Zak pinched himself, then pinched himself again. Nothing had changed. There was only one thing for it. If he really was still dreaming, he'd just dream for longer and longer. He'd carry on dreaming and enjoy everything that was happening to him.

'This is your life from now on, Zed Dog.' Tony winked at Zak, his pearly white teeth glimmering in the light above his plate of paella. 'Let's enjoy it.'

Before flying back to England, there was only one thing left to do. El Clasico, the biggest rivalry in Spanish football – perhaps even world football. FC Barcelona v Real Madrid, live at the Camp Nou. Eleven of the world's best footballers against eleven of the world's best footballers. And Zak, not only watching on from the players' lounge as guest of honour, but performing on the pitch at half-time!

The atmosphere was electric. The Camp Nou was packed, tens of thousands of fans rising high into the sky until they were so far away they could barely see the players. A small pocket of white swayed to and fro in the top corner of the stadium: the away end. Everywhere else was a sea of blue and red. The air was thick with anticipation. The fans didn't just want Barcelona to win; they wanted them to put on a show.

From Zak's angle, he could see everything clearly. He felt so close that he could almost reach out and touch the very players he'd seen the day before on the training ground. He could smell the grass, freshly watered by the stadium's sophisticated sprinkler system until it was so perfectly green that it couldn't possibly be natural. On such a surface, the ball zipped around. Barcelona's opening goal was met with roars from the home fans and a sea of white handkerchiefs from the away fans. With thirty minutes on the clock and Zak absorbed in the game, Tony told him it was time. They marched into the depths of the stadium with Zak's dad, Zak eager to hurry. With a capacity of 99,354 and not a seat going spare, it'd be by far the biggest live crowd Zak had ever performed in front of. It felt like Redwood shopping centre multiplied by a million.

He changed into his new Panther Sports kit and laced up his brand new golden Free 10 boots. There was still time. He focused on his ball and rolled it from foot to foot, getting his feet used to the feel of it. He took three deep breaths, as he always did before a performance, then shifted his gaze to the pitch. 'Showtime,' he muttered.

The Barcelona and Real Madrid players went one way into the tunnel, climbing the steps in various states of tiredness. Zak went the other, a spring in every step. Some of the Barcelona players recognised Zak and stopped to clap him on the back on their way to the dressing room. Gerard Pique even fist-bumped him.

They knew who he was.

The players he pretended to be on the Xbox were now greeting him. Zak puffed his chest out in pride. The nerves disappeared, replaced by confidence. If the Barcelona players knew him, what did he have to worry about?

Ball in hand, he walked past the famous chapel on the right hand side of the tunnel, imagining all of the famous players who'd prayed there over the years. It'd been blessed by Pope John Paul II himself. So many legends had walked this walk. His studs clanged against the steps. He was getting lower and lower and then there it was, the entrance to the pitch. A distant rectangle of green grass that got bigger with every step. And then the noise hit him. He'd never heard anything like it. This wasn't the same noise that he'd experienced from the stands. It was the sound of 99,354 people, all directing their own noise at the pitch. Their cheers and chants and laughter all blurred into one ball of noise that blasted against Zak. The hairs on his arms stood up. It was exhilarating.

Before he knew it, he was in the centre circle of one of the most famous stadiums in world football. 99,354 pairs of eyes were on him. The ground was full to capacity.

He turned in a full circle, taking in the crowd, enjoying their excitement and then embracing the hush that fell on him.

And then the music started playing. The stadium manager had chosen 'Waka Waka' by Shakira. It wasn't Zak's choice but at least it had a beat. He could work to it. He bared his teeth, readjusted his headband and spread his weight evenly. If he was going to put on a show he'd need to be perfectly balanced.

His every move followed by FC Barcelona's official camera crew, Zak flicked the ball up from the sole of his foot and caught it on his head. All of his focus was on the ball, but he couldn't help hearing gasps over the din of the music. He knew he'd impressed the crowd, and that knowledge helped him ease into his performance. 'The pressure is on, you feel it, but you've got it all, believe it,' Shakira sang. The words couldn't have been more relevant. For three minutes he was flawless. His combos were immaculate, his execution spot-on. From his head stall he did his much-practised trick of kissing the ball and then rolling it back onto his neck. Lifting his arms by his sides he swirled around in circles, enjoying the dizzying sensation and playing up to the crowd. Now they weren't just gasping but cheering too. He dropped down, the ball still on his neck. Zak needed to keep his body perfectly straight so the ball remained balanced. Just one slip and he'd drop it. His muscles tensed. His arms shivered. Carefully, he lowered himself into a press-up, then a second one. Applause. They were applauding him! Zak could taste the green grass from down here, the hallowed turf of FC Barcelona. So much fresher than the Redwood Rovers pitch of mud and dog poo. The very same grass that Messi tasted whenever he was fouled. Half raising himself from the press-ups, he then tugged at his shirt. The shirt responded, inching over his headband and revealing the skin of his back to the crowd. Even though the music still played, Zak sensed the silence. They were all watching him. He couldn't make them out. They were just one big blur of red and blue but they were there. Another tug. The shirt came off, leaving the ball triumphantly on his neck. The sound from the crowd came at him with all of the force of an aeroplane leaving a runway. For just a second, he allowed himself to bask in the glory of their cheers. Then, the big finale. The ball and his body were moving as one. 'Today's your day,' sang Shakira. 'I feel it, you paved the way.' The ball soared through the air. This was all about timing. If he followed the ball's arc and caught it at exactly the right moment it'd be perfect. He readied his heel, leaving a ball-shaped space between the boot and his bum. At the first feel of the ball he clenched heel and bum together. The ball stopped dead. Now came the more difficult part. Focusing on a spot of grass three yards in front of him, Zak thrust forward his arms and somersaulted forward. His body flew through the air, the ball glued to his body. He just needed to land it and then he was done . . . his entire weight had to be caught in his free left leg. He dangled it above the ground and then bent it forward. As his body met the turf he hopped forward, struggling to hold the weight. His left leg screamed at him. *Please*, he willed, *please*. It worked. He came to a stop, standing with the ball still between his heel and bum. Now he saw the crowd. They'd risen to their feet and were whooping and hollering. Egged on, he released the ball and volleyed it high into the rafters of the stadium. Their cheers came even louder. Thousands waved white handkerchiefs at him in support. Camera phones flashed. And all because of him.

Zak had never felt a buzz like it.

He wanted to bottle the moment up and feel this way forever. He was invincible. A star. A king. Nothing could stop him.

Nothing except the two teams returning from their dressing rooms and one impatient referee, that is.

YouTube subscribers: 722,037
Instagram followers: 589,972
Twitter followers: 106,783

The Barcelona footage excited Zak's fans like nothing else. There had been so much footage captured that there was plenty of content ready to be released. And when Panther Sports released their own advert with Zak, his social media channels blew up in popularity.

'YO THIS KID IS BIG' @megaMovements
'MAD TEKK – ZAK IS THE FUTURE YOU KNOW' @TopBinsForFun
'SOMEONE PUT THIS KID OUT HE'S ON FIRE 🔥🔥🔥' @TheEnforcer123
'How can man be skilling up Barcelona players like that?!' @MessiMagic973

There was no time to rest. It didn't matter that they had lots of videos stored up. There was always a chance to create more.

Tony was spending more time around Zak's house. There was no better sign that Zak was doing well. His skills were making Tony money, and if Tony was making money then Zak and his dad were also making money. Hundreds of thousands of pounds of it. Enough to no longer need to worry about the bills on the kitchen table. So much that they could afford to fix the draughty window and the dodgy boiler. There were even two new widescreen televisions and a comprehensive sound system. Not that Zak had any idea of the exact sums involved. His dad handled everything. That way Zak only had to worry about his skills.

One afternoon, following a particularly intense freestyle session, Tony approached Zak. 'Zed Dog, what are you doing this evening?'

Zak could tell from the man's tone that Tony already knew what he had planned for the evening, but he played along anyway. 'I'm going training with Redwood, just like I do every Tuesday evening when we've done enough filming. And I know we've done enough this week.'

Even though Tony grimaced, his teeth still glistened. 'I don't think that's a good idea,' he replied. Zak's dad stared at the floor. 'We're on the way to stardom,' Tony continued. 'It'd be stupid to risk everything because you want to play football with your mates. What if you get injured?'

Redwood Rovers had been Zak's life for so many years. He loved playing football, loved the freedom that the game brought him. It had been his identity. It was what he did with his best mate. It was what he'd looked forward to every Saturday. And now he was being asked to give it up and put everything into his life as a YouTuber.

Zak understood what Tony was saying. His words made perfect sense. It would be stupid for Zak to lose everything by getting injured. Just like it would have been stupid for Zak to carry on going to school after his beating. He knew just how social media stars are quickly made, but even more quickly forgotten. That was why he always had to make so many videos so regularly. He had to keep creating content so his followers wouldn't forget him.

Football was everything. But this was more.

An injury would be devastating. It would ruin everything.

'Listen to Mr Curtis, son,' Zak's dad said from behind the agent. He was still looking at the floor, as if he didn't truly believe the words that were coming out of his mouth. 'It's only short term. Just while we make the most of your Barcelona video.'

Tony remained the model of confidence, his tanned biceps resting over his torso, his teeth glimmering as always. 'This is about aspiration,' he said. That word again. *Aspiration.* Zak's mind flashed back to the beating. Tony had used that very same word to convince him to stop going to school. 'Why muck about with your mates when you can be a star? People around the world would give anything to be in your shoes. Forget Redwood Rovers. You're a big fish in a small pond there. Forget football full stop. The money is in YouTube now. YouTubers are the new footballers. YouTubers are the new rock stars. Don't risk it all for a bit of fun with your mates.'

Zak knew he was going to have no choice in the matter.

Reluctantly he reached for the phone and punched in Mr Jones's number.

YouTube subscribers: 898,306
Instagram followers: 676,349
Twitter followers: 132,222

Occasionally, Zak wondered what his mates were up to. He thought of Marcus and Josh practising their secret handshake, of Chris talking about his friends in year 11, of Mr Jones preaching about discipline. Mostly, he thought of Chloe and what she was doing that very moment. Had she found someone new? Who was her strike partner now? Was she still lethal on *FIFA*?

Every time his thoughts wandered, he tried his hardest to snap out of it. They were moments of weakness. That was his old life. That's what Zak told himself over and over. His old life was gone. Thinking about it wouldn't change anything.

Now he lived a new life. A life of fanatical support from his followers, of luxury and VIP treatment, of success, of being a somebody, not a nobody like all of those people that he had left behind.

Now he had new mates. His dad had been concerned that without school and football he'd have nobody to hang around with. And so Tony encouraged him to start hanging out with Baller B and two of his other clients, Z2K and ItsMintThat. They had plenty in common, Tony told them. Most importantly, though, they were all powerful. Not like Chloe, Tony had sneered. She didn't even have 100 followers!

Zak was learning a lot about power.

When he uploaded his very first video, he did it because he thought it was cool. He enjoyed freestyling and wanted to share it with the world. But as he uploaded more and more, he began to crave more power. That's the thing with followers. There were always more. His follower count was never enough. There were always more people to engage with, more views to get, more likes. And the more he got, the more powerful he felt.

It was addictive.

Hanging out with Baller B didn't sound like his idea of fun. Off camera he had been quiet and evasive, almost as if he was afraid of human contact. Zak wasn't looking forward to becoming friends with him. But he was looking forward to all of the shoutouts from Baller B's social media content he knew he'd get as a result. To becoming more powerful. So he agreed.

He soon found out that they had nothing in common. It seemed to Zak that his new friends spent a lot of time filming each other doing . . . nothing much at all. Mostly they lounged in the plush bean bags of Tony's games room and scrolled their phones relentlessly. It was no wonder Baller B's skills were average at best. They never enjoyed kickabouts together. Any attempt at a real life conversation hung in the air. Only questions about followers and content gained responses. Stories were told of videos that had attracted millions of views, of fans crashing the internet by clicking through to links shared, of the money they were paid to endorse products.

Zak laughed along with them, even though he was the subject of many of their jokes. After all, he was the only one who didn't have a million followers on any social media platform. And he was the youngest.

Z2K was the worst. He was a child in a teenager's body. His limbs flailed wildly as he moved. His teeth stuck out from his mouth. Hair stuck up in random places all over his head. His speciality lay in creating humiliating videos, and with Zak he'd found a new target. On one particularly horrible occasion milk, eggs and flour were all poured over Zak to the delight of all Z2K's followers. Zak hated being the butt of the jokes. Yet he also knew that every time Z2K tagged him in a social media post he gained new followers. It made him more powerful.

Zak tried to fight back, but he swiftly found that making jokes at the expense of his new friends didn't go down well. If Zak laughed at Baller B's obsession with his phone the room was struck by a frosty silence. If Zak squirted water at Z2K he was given a slap. Social media stars, Zak soon learnt, weren't used to criticism and so he stayed quiet, forever scrolling on his phone as a way of fitting in.

The moments of weakness became more common. As the weeks with his new friends passed, he increasingly found his thumb forever hovering over the Redwood Legends group.

The group had been inactive for ages. But what if he was to just send a message? Only now, he realised just how much he missed his old friends. Hanging around with Baller B and his cronies wasn't freedom. Running over to the park with Chloe and joking around with Josh, Chris and Marcus was. Launching attack after attack for Redwood, changing the game in an instant was beautiful. Had he been just like Baller B and his cronies with them? Had all of his focus on followers and social media pushed them away? Now that he no longer hung out with them, he realised just how much he missed them.

But what good would they do him? They couldn't get him the followers that Baller B or Z2K or ItsMintThat could. They'd only hinder his path to stardom. In those moments of confusion, his phone proved a welcome distraction. These days it was always red hot. After meeting up in Barcelona, Cristiano Ronaldo had continued to comment on Zak's videos. When people saw Ronaldo commenting, thousands more jumped in. They commented on his videos, sent him DMs and asked him for signed merchandise.

Some of the more famous ones even asked Zak to appear in their own videos. Having Zak, they reasoned, would help them to attract more fans. The clubs they played for followed their lead, inviting Zak to games and giving him the VIP treatment while encouraging him to show his support for them.

Every day there was a new shoot, a new media commitment, a new business opportunity. The Panther Sports advert led to sponsorship deals with clothing brands, restaurant chains, a mobile phone network, a watch brand, a camera manufacturer, even his own fresh noodle partner. Each deal earnt more money but also came with more requests. With his star ever growing, he began to appear on television shows. At first they used him as a local news story, but soon enough he was performing on the television shows. Really, he found it was no different to usual. He no longer felt pressure. Everything came already programmed. Robotic.

Tony rubbed his hands together in glee at every new deal he was able to make. With the offers rolling in and his followers shooting up, Tony announced that the time was right for Zak to release his very own merchandise. He'd already decided on the name for the merchandise: #KeepItTekk. A clothing designer had been hired to work on the first drop of merch. Zak winced when he saw the designs. #KeepItTekk was splashed loudly across all of the designs, but the colours of the clothes and snapbacks were all dull.

'Are there any colourful pieces of merchandise?' he asked. Surely Tony knew that he liked bright football boots? Surely Tony knew that he always wore bright t-shirts? But Tony only laughed.

'A lot of research has gone into these products. The people who have designed this are experts. They work with the very best. They know what sells.'

'But do I have to wear them?' Zak asked.

There was only one answer to that question. The first outing of his #KeepItTekk range came while performing on *Good Morning Britain*. Millions tuned in to ITV and saw him perform in front of the backdrop of St. Paul's cathedral. They all saw him then sit on the sofa with Piers Little-Brown and Amy Redman. They all heard as he was asked about his clothing range and announced that it was sick, just as Tony had told him to say. And then they all went out and bought it.

The first merchandise drop sold out within minutes of Zak coming off air.

Zak felt privileged to be doing what he was doing. Who else his age had their own clothing range, celebrity mates, appearances on national television and hundreds of thousands of followers? It didn't matter that there was barely enough time left for Zak to film his own content. It didn't matter that he was having less and less of a say in what happened each day.

All that mattered was his success. Every spare moment had to be about his success. Tony told him that he needed to become a brand. He needed to be bigger than YouTube. The more places his face could be, the more likely that was to happen.

There was no time to be tired. Time being tired was time that could be spent building his brand. Zak soon learned to never tell Tony when he was feeling worn out. Even as he went from shoot to shoot, television programme to radio station, all the while losing valuable training time to perfect his new tricks. Shooting was knackering but he couldn't miss out on training. Sometimes he'd even return home close to midnight and have to grab an hour of practice. His dad told him to go easy but how could he? He had to keep on improving. He had to keep on producing even better moves and even better videos to keep on riding The Snowball. There was nothing else he could do: he just had to grin and bear it.

This was his new life. It was sick. It was everything that he had ever wanted.

That's what Tony kept on telling him, at least.

YouTube subscribers: 918,306
Instagram followers: 701,230
Twitter followers: 137,230

Zak woke with a start. He rolled over and checked his alarm clock. 03:04.

How long had he been asleep? He must have had four hours. Well, two sets of two hours. Was that enough?

He unlocked his phone and checked all of his social media channels. Followers gained on all of them. Good.

What about the comments? He scrolled through the new ones and liked a few.

Back to sleep.

But only briefly. Barely had he closed his eyes when he awoke sweating. 03:52. Not to worry. It was just a bad dream.

He unlocked his phone again. Follower increases again. Good. Not as much as before, but still increases.

04:01. Not much point in going back to sleep. The sun was going to rise soon. Getting up now would give him extra time to practise skills for a new video. It'd be his only chance. With all of the media commitments and business events coming up that day, Zak needed to make the most of every minute.

Even when it was only him and the birds awake.

Through bleary eyes, Zak pulled on his training kit. He tiptoed downstairs so as not to wake his dad and poured himself a glass of water. After downing that, he grabbed a cereal bar. That was breakfast out of the way.

The early morning was his. He had several hours until his dad woke up, and a bit longer from then until his first commitment.

Zak set up his camera facing the area he was going to work in. Leaving it on a tripod enabled him to capture any fresh combos he was going to pull off. It wasn't as high quality as when Nat filmed him, but if he wasn't filming what he was doing at all times then it was a waste.

There was no time to be tired. With every kick, Zak repeated the same phrase in his head.

You can't sleep on success.

You can't sleep on success.

You can't sleep on success.

You can't sleep—

YouTube subscribers: 931,464
Instagram followers: 710,049
Twitter followers: 146,494

There was no time to be tired but Zak *was* tired. He yawned his way through the days, surviving on sugar hits from the simple carbohydrates he was fed as he was rushed from commitment to commitment. And Zak wasn't just tired in mind. He was also tired in body. He was working so hard, performing so often, that it was having an effect on his body.

One lunchtime he stole fifteen minutes of practice in his back yard before Tony arrived to take him to a photo shoot with the *Radio Times*. He wanted to work on his mouse traps, a classic moved used in panna to fool an opponent. There was an idea to play panna against members of the public and Zak was well aware he needed to brush up his skills to shoot a good video. He worked on both feet, cramming as much as he could into the short time. And then he heard the raised voices. They were coming from the house. He stopped in his tracks and craned his neck to the noise. He could just about make out his dad's voice. The other sounded like Tony. What was happening? Nervous, he rushed back inside.

The two men were standing close to each other. His dad had risen to his full height, his hands poised. Tony was panting, his permanently tanned face a shade of red. They had been staring at each other. When they saw Zak they both wheeled around, as if they'd been caught by a teacher doing something wrong.

'See, look at him. He's fine!' For a moment Tony Curtis hadn't looked like Tony Curtis. Now, however, his teeth glimmered as always. His face was a brilliant shade of tan. A Rolex weighed lightly against his wrist. 'Tired!' he scoffed. 'You're fine, aren't you, Zak?'

'Yes,' Zak lied. He was used to saying what he was supposed to say.

'Get your stuff, son. We'll leave in two minutes,' his dad said, motioning for him to go upstairs. This wasn't a time to argue. Zak walked up the stairs, then paused as soon as he was out of sight.

'I don't like it, Mr Curtis,' he heard his dad's voice start up again. This time he spoke in a hushed tone. Knowing that Zak would soon be back, his words tumbled out. 'Zak's not his normal self. He needs to go easier. He's going to burn out.' Burn out! How could his dad say that to Tony? Sure, Zak was tired. But he'd rather be tired than miss out on being a superstar.

'Listen, we've just got a few more commitments,' Tony replied. 'After the second drop of his merchandise he can go easier for a couple of weeks. Get his energy levels back.'

'I hope you're right,' his dad replied. 'I'm absolutely loving this journey, Mr Curtis. We all are. You've been brilliant for us. But I don't want to risk his health. It's not healthy to be tired all of the time.' Zak was taken aback. He thought he'd hid the stolen yawns and the powernaps. But how could he rest? Not when the other YouTuber freestylers were putting out content so regularly. Zak constantly monitored what his rivals were doing. He was ahead of them, engaging more followers, putting out better videos, and he needed to stay ahead of them. Still, there were lessons he took from his rivals. The way @Swazzy created a trademark dance move as a goal celebration. The audacity of @TopBinsTim in nutmegging members of the public. The breadth of content from @Pingsville that saw her conduct tutorials, esports, skills, comedy routines and interviews.

A few weeks passed and still the commitments came. The second merchandise drop sold out and a third was scheduled. His time became so squeezed that Zak took to freestyling when he brushed his teeth and ate his meals. On the rare occasions that he was able to have a proper session, he worked manically.

He'd mastered the mouse trap. His panna video had been viewed millions of times. Now he was working on a trick shots skit. With the bin placed against the back wall of the yard, he practised over and over. It was just like he used to do with Chloe at the park. They'd stand either side of the play area and attempt to pass the ball through the tyre. Back then he played football because he loved it. Not because he had to. Back then he hung out with Chloe because she was his best mate. Not like the new people he hung out with. He let the ball rebound off the wall and drop into the corner of the yard. He missed Chloe. He missed football. He allowed his memories to take him away, to imagine what it would be like to be running through another defence in his Redwood Rovers kit, playing one-twos with Chloe before unleashing an unstoppable effort into the corner.

No. He had to stop thinking about his past. That wasn't his reality. That was his old life. He took the ball with renewed energy. Another lobbed pass with his right leg. Another miss. There was a reason they called them trick shots. They weren't easy. Other YouTubers spent hours filming to get the one shot they needed. It always looked like they did the trick first time but that was never the truth. With every miss, Zak became more determined. He cursed, then ran to get the ball back and place it on the same spot and try all over again. His legs screamed at him. They wanted to rest. They were so sore. He couldn't even feel his left leg. But his mind willed him on. He had to do this. He'd started and now he had to finish, otherwise it would be a wasted training session. He didn't have time to waste. With the ball on the spot and the bin in his sights, he planted his left foot on the ground and shot with his right. Foot met ball. As the ball floated from his foot he followed through with the movement. From nowhere, a sharp pain shot down his leg. He cried out in surprise, no longer worrying about the ball. It couldn't take his weight. Gingerly, Zak placed the right foot on the ground. It was like a chemical reaction. The ground pushed back and Zak hopped on his left foot. This wasn't good. Supposing he'd done something serious? There'd be no more television appearances or skills videos or brand deals. Everything would be gone in a kick. He'd never known pain like it. He'd never been injured before.

'What's happened?' His dad had heard the scream and rushed out of the house. Concern was etched across his face.

'My leg!' Zak wailed. 'It's agony.'

'Where does it hurt?'

'Here.' Zak pointed to the back of his thigh. 'My hamstring.' In his panic he remembered Harry Kane's hamstring injury. It was so bad that he'd needed surgery. Zak couldn't have surgery. He couldn't afford to. So much time away would ruin him.

'How did you do it?' His dad took hold of his right hamstring, pressing gently against it and talking as calmly as possible.

'Just by kicking the ball . . . what do you think it is?'

'It's okay. You've probably just pulled your muscle. I'll let Mr Curtis know.'

'No.' If Tony knew then he might pull Zak out of the TV interview he was scheduled to do that evening. 'I'll be fine.' He'd still be able to perform a few basic tricks. He had to. The show was being aired in primetime. It could really boost his following.

His dad sighed. 'I'm going to tell him. Mr Curtis deserves to know. But let me see what I can do for you.' With that his dad disappeared upstairs and returned minutes later carrying something in his right hand. 'This is what we all used back in our day,' he explained as he handed over a faded white tube. 'It's a bit old now but should still work. Always used to do the trick on me.'

'What is it?' Zak asked. 'Is it legal?' His dad laughed at the question.

'Is it legal?' he repeated, tears of laughter replacing the concern in his eyes. 'Son, it's only Deep Heat. What do you think it is? Here,' he squirted a pea-sized amount onto his fingers. 'Try this.'

His dad reached for the hamstring and massaged the affected area with the clear liquid. Zak's skin burned, but it wasn't a painful burn. The smell was fierce, a fresh, minty aroma that opened his nostrils and went deep into his lungs. 'It's just a quick fix,' he added. 'Good for minor injuries. It increases the blood flow to the area it's applied. It helps to manage pain.' Zak pocketed the rest of the tube. His hamstring still twanged with pain but the pain was more bearable. He could put weight on the leg. If it still hurt later he could always rub in more Deep Heat. Yes, the tube would definitely be useful. If it helped to relieve pain then maybe it could help ease the soreness his legs felt every day. And then he'd be able to train even better!

When Tony arrived at the house later that afternoon to take Zak and his dad to the TV studios, he was holding a wad of papers.

'Sign this, Zed Dog, my man.' It was a contract, another one. Pages and pages with clauses and terms and conditions. Tony held it out for him, his beaming smile inviting Zak to scribble on the line.

There were always new contracts.

Zak barely bothered to read them anymore. If Tony wanted him to sign them, he knew it was best to sign.

Zak took the pen and scrawled his name across the dotted lines. Tony flicked the pages, directing Zak to sign on another three dotted lines.

With the signing finished, Tony put his arm around Zak. 'Nice one, Zed Dog,' he said. 'We've just insured your legs for ten million pounds.'

'What?' Zak couldn't believe what he'd just heard. How could anybody's legs be worth so much money?

'That's right,' Tony continued. 'Your legs are your wands. Think what would have happened to Harry Potter if he didn't have his wand. He wouldn't have become a billionaire, that's for sure.'

Zak was too stunned to even ask Tony whether he'd actually read the Harry Potter books.

'Your Dad told me your legs were feeling sore,' Tony continued. 'I brought some painkillers with me that you can take before going on air. I'm sure it's nothing, but now we're always prepared for the worst. Your legs will make us billions, just like Harry Potter's wand made him billions, but at the very worst we'll now make millions.' Tony rubbed his hands together and smiled at Zak's dad, who moved his lips in a cross between a smile and a grimace.

'Shall we do this then?' Tony asked.

Determined, Zak nodded. The TV interview would be broadcast to millions. His face would be on television screens up and down the country. The more places he was seen, the brighter his star would shine. He couldn't let a hamstring stop him.

Zak followed Tony to his chauffeur-driven car.

Showtime.

YouTube subscribers: 1,000,430
Instagram followers: 780,204
Twitter followers: 161,434

'Yes, yes. You know the score, it's Zak here. I've got something very special to say. I can't believe I'm going to say it because it's mad. When I first started off I never thought I'd get to this stage. I've just hit ONE MILLION followers! Wow. Mad. Look at this gold plaque YouTube gave me as a reward! I want to thank each and every one of you for watching, liking and subscribing. You guys drive me on to create even better content. I couldn't have done it without you. So before I go, I've just got one thing to say. Keep it tekk.'

Zak turned from the camera and flicked up a ball. He caught it underneath his jumper, then dropped it back to his feet. A couple of round the worlds to start, then up to the shoulders. It was time to drop all the classics that had got him into this position. The fans would love it. Then, the big finale. Zak caught the ball on his neck, did a couple of spins, then pulled off his #KeepItTekk hoodie while the ball stayed on his back, totally motionless. Zak turned his jumper so the hood was almost on the floor and the hem was in his hands, then flicked the ball into the fabric. He flung the ball and jumper over his shoulder as if it was a sack, then turned and winked at the camera. 'Tekky.' He took three paces forward, then doubled back to the camera. 'Don't forget to like, subscribe and turn on notifications, yeah? Here's to the next million.'

Nat stopped recording and Tony emerged from behind the camera.

'Wow. Wow. Wow. That was great. Do you see what I mean about energy? When you speak with that much energy on camera it's so engaging. Your fans are going to love it.'

Zak slumped onto the garden chair in total exhaustion, still clutching onto his gold plaque. His million-follower video had to be special. He'd given it everything. Cautiously, he reached for his hamstring. Nothing. The Deep Heat had done the job. Zak had to give it to his dad, it was good stuff.

They wasted no time in getting the video uploaded. It was just a simple video to give thanks. Jazz had it ready in only twenty minutes, her spindly fingers moving like rockets over her Apple Mac. A disorientating zoom into Zak to start with, flame emojis, memes and a backing track with a big beat were all added. So was a link to buy the latest #KeepItTekk merchandise and to follow Zak's other channels.

Just as they had all predicted, the fans loved it.

'YOUR VIDEOS ARE TOO SICK AND I KNOW YOUR NEW ONES WILL BE DOPE' @NinjaBaller
'LIKE THS IS YOU'VE BEEN WITH ZAK SINCE THE START!!!' @FrankirbyIsLife
'CONGRATULATIONS! YOUR VIDEOS INSPIRE ME TO GO FOR MY GOALS 👑' @BabySharkxo
'TEAM TEKKERS YO 💯' @SmokeyFadez
'WE'RE WITH YOU ALL THE WAY ZAK. YOU THE BEST FREESTYLER OUT IN THIS JOINT' @skillzguru

As the comments rolled in, Zak's eyes watered. This video had never been about views or likes or getting new followers. It was a video for the fans. Hearing stories of how Zak had inspired his followers to achieve their dreams was incredible. He had done this. It was all worth it.

And as the comments came in, the views and new follower counts increased and increased.

Baller B and ItsMintThat sent their followers to watch the video, with Z2K sharing it and congratulating Zak in one of his videos.

There were comments from Ronaldo, Ronaldinho and Jadon Sancho.

And there was even a DM from the agent of Abou Trabt! Zak's favourite footballer of all time wanted to invite him to a party that he was holding in Redwood the following evening. The agent said how Abou loved Zak's videos and wanted to hang with him.

Excitedly, Zak told his dad and insisted he had to go. It wasn't every day you got invited to Abou Trabt's house! His dad told him he was sure it'd be fine, so long as it was okay with Tony.

But when he dialled the call, something in his face filled Zak with worry. He watched with growing unease as his dad explained the situation, but his expression didn't improve. Something was wrong.

'What? What's he saying?' Zak couldn't work out what was taking so long. His dad signed off and hung up.

'Sorry, son,' he began. 'Tony says you have to film with Baller B and Z2K tomorrow. He wants to build on the momentum of your celebration video.'

'But, but, but,' Zak replied. 'It's Abou Trabt!'

'I know, son. The problem is that nobody on social media knows who Abou Trabt is. Mr Curtis pointed out that he doesn't even have 10,000 followers. He called him an egg. I'm not sure what he meant by that.'

'It's when you're new on social media, when your profile picture is just an egg on Twitter,' Zak explained. The words came out of his mouth but he wasn't concentrating on them. All that he could think of was Abou Trabt and his missed opportunity.

'I'm sure you'll be able to hang out with Abou Trabt in a couple of months when you get a little less busy,' his dad tried to reassure him.

The words were hot air. Meaningless. Because in a couple of months there would be a new goal, a new follower count to aim for. There was never going to be a time to slow down.

He would never be less busy.

YouTube subscribers: 1,005,948
Instagram followers: 783,342
Twitter followers: 161,985

MILLION UP FOR MAGIC MAN ZAK
By Cynthia Johnson

Teenage sensation Zak Oxden (pictured) has passed another milestone on his path to social media superstardom.

The former Redwood Rovers striker from King's Lane, Redwood, first uploaded a video of his skills six months ago. That video was shared far and wide, and now every single one of Zak's videos is watched by a global audience.

His talent has been recognised by international footballers, famous brands and celebrities. Recently, Zak has even transcended football freestyle, successfully launching his #KeepItTekk clothes brand.

With the world at his feet, the sky is the limit for local boy Zak. All at The Redwood Review wish the best of luck to Zak, who unfortunately was unavailable for comment due to his hectic schedule.

Zak's agent, Tony Curtis, said the following: 'Everyone wants a piece of Zak. As I'm sure you'll appreciate, he's on an incredibly busy schedule right now, but rest assured he wants to thank the entire town of Redwood and also The Redwood Review *for all of their support of Zak. Zak loves living in Redwood.'*

Follow Zak's videos on @therealTekkerZak

YouTube subscribers: 1,151,464
Instagram followers: 810,049
Twitter followers: 176,494

Incoming call. Caller ID: Chloe Smith.

Zak had been checking up on the statistics for his latest video when Chloe's name flashed up on his screen.

Chloe.

He hadn't heard from her since that incident after training.

Could she have forgiven him?

Without a second thought, Zak answered.

'Chloe, what's up?' In the corner of the room, Tony's ears pricked up. He immediately stopped what he was doing and paid full attention to Zak and the phone in his hand.

'Zak, you've got to help us.' Chloe was never one for letting emotions get in the way of things. She was straight to the point, as if nothing had happened between the two of them.

'It's Adam. He's been replacing you up front. He's been playing well and scoring, but last night in training he twisted his ankle and he's going to be out injured for a couple of weeks.'

'That sucks,' Zak responded. He hadn't realised how much he missed the sound of his best mate's voice.

'Look, just listen, okay?' she cut him off. 'We made it to the county cup final. Not that you're bothered about that. You probably forgot we were even playing in a cup.'

'I hadn't!' he said truthfully. If she'd said that a few weeks ago she would have been right. But not anymore . . .

'Listen!' Chloe cut Zak off before he could defend himself. 'The cup final is this weekend.' Zak felt Tony inch closer to him. He was so close his ear was almost next to Zak's. 'And now we don't have anyone who can play up front with me. The registration deadline has passed so we can't sign someone new. The only player left is Gareth.'

'Who's Gareth?'

'Exactly! It's Mr Jones's son. He's so bad that Mr Jones doesn't even let him train with us. He just signed him on in case of an emergency. And now we have an emergency! So can you sort us out? It's just one game. You can play one game for us and then that'll be it. You can go back to your life as a social media superstar and forget that any of us ever existed. But please, for old times' sake. For your mates. Come on, Zak.'

If only she knew how much he thought of old times. At first the pangs had come rarely. He'd wondered how Chloe or Chris or Josh or Marcus were doing. He'd pictured them alongside him. Just for a few seconds, then he'd shaken them away. It was better to forget them. But more recently the pangs came for longer. They became harder to shake. He began to yearn for the time when he could dribble on a football pitch without a camera following him. When he could go to any party that he wanted to. When he laughed and joked with his friends. His real friends. And now that old life had reappeared from nowhere. He wanted to go back and live it all over again. Filming gave him a rush, getting millions of likes gave him an exhilaration like no other, but nothing could ever beat the freedom that came from running around a football pitch with not a care in the world other than getting three points. In his new reality everything he did had to have a purpose. Everything was aimed at increasing his brand or gaining followers. He wanted to forget all of that, to have a break for just 90 minutes, to avoid his every moment being managed, to do something for the sheer enjoyment rather than because it had a greater purpose.

But he never had a chance.

'I'd love—' he began. Before he was able to finish his sentence, the phone was snatched from his grip. Tony sneered at the name on the screen and hung up the call. The confusion at his disappearing phone turned to anger. Could he have no say over any little thing in his life?

'What are you doing!' he exclaimed, feeling the flames of anger burning even hotter.

'It's the right thing, Zak,' he said calmly, his diamonded fingers glinting in the artificial light of the living room. 'You can't even risk one match. What purpose will it have? You won't get any success from that.'

'I've got millions of followers,' Zak protested. 'My own clothing range. Brand deals. I've got everything you ever

227

wanted for me. All I want is one weekend!' He was shouting now and he didn't care who heard.

'Calm down,' his dad rushed to his side and put his arm around his shoulder. 'We'll sort something.'

'And besides,' Tony added triumphantly. 'You're fully booked up this weekend. We've got that Perfect Whites toothpaste advert to film. You can't possibly miss that.'

'I can!' Zak screamed back. 'I can and I will.'

'Zak, you don't know what you're saying.' His dad ushered him onto the sofa. 'Have a time out. Give it a couple of minutes.'

'Give it as long as you like,' Tony added. 'You've just got a few more events and then you can have a rest. There's absolutely no chance you can miss the Perfect Whites shoot, though. You signed a contract with them, remember? Breach of contract is a serious crime.' The flames roared inside him. Zak ran up the stairs and locked himself in his bedroom. He flung himself onto the bed and screamed into his pillow with all of his rage.

This was his new life. It was sick. It was everything that he had ever wanted.

YouTube subscribers: 1,296,483
Instagram followers: 926,435
Twitter followers: 181,432

02:29. Everything was okay. It was just a nightmare.

Zak had been running. He was running as fast as he could, but it wasn't enough. The Snowball was going to catch him. It was getting closer and closer and then it was on top of him, crushing him and pulling him under, down into the depths of freezing cold nothingness. *Help!* Zak screamed. *Help!* But there was nobody there.

He'd woken up with the sheets soaked in sweat.

It was a regular occurrence in recent weeks. The days were fine. Zak had enough distractions to keep him focused. But the nights were tough. That's when the stresses and strains of his new life crept in. Alone with his thoughts, the pressure became overwhelming. Constantly, Zak found himself waking to check on his follower numbers.

It wasn't becoming an obsession. It was already way past that.

He wasn't sleeping enough. How could he when there weren't enough hours in the day? The 4am rises had become part of Zak's routine.

It should have made him tired, but when Zak shut his eyes at night he was plagued by bad dreams. They came and devoured him, gripped him in their clutches and spat him out into a sweat-soaked bed.

How long could he go on like this?

As long as it took to make it. He had no other option.

Thoughts of disconnecting came and went. They floated around, inviting him to take a minute to himself. It couldn't hurt, could it?

There was never the chance. The commitments were too great, and if there were no commitments then Tony was always monitoring him and making sure he was building the brand.

In a parallel universe, Zak knew that he was preparing for the cup final. He fantasised about getting ready for the big game with his old mates from Redwood Rovers. He could picture them all laughing and joking, then getting serious as Mr Jones led them through their team talk.

What he'd give to be there that weekend.

What he'd give to have 90 minutes where he wouldn't need to be connected.

Zak couldn't remember how it felt to not be plugged in to this world. He tried to imagine there being no pressure on him to constantly engage with his fans. With a smile, he thought back to a time when he didn't have to create and upload a new video every single day. A time when he didn't have to parade himself in front of that stupid camera, just so people he'd never met and would never meet could comment with their emojis and click that like button and that follow button.

03:12.

What was the point of his fame? What good was it if it kept him awake all night and took away his freedom? What was the point in being a star if he couldn't do as he pleased?

03:15.

Forty-five minutes until his alarm was set to go off for his morning training session. He wouldn't get back to sleep now. There was only one thing for it.

Wearily, Zak opened his wardrobe and reached for his training kit.

There was no time to be tired.

YouTube subscribers: 1,351,235
Instagram followers: 952,493
Twitter followers: 191,411

'Perfect Whites is the world's third biggest toothpaste brand, don't you know? Quite impressive.' His dad grinned.

'Right,' Zak muttered. He was too tired to feel enthusiastic. How could he get excited about a toothpaste commercial?

'Sometimes I have to sit back and think how amazing this whole experience is. You've done this, Zak. To think that Perfect Whites has asked my boy to appear in an advert.' He shook his head in disbelief, then reached forward and touched Tony on the shoulder. 'Thank you, Mr Curtis. Thank you.'

For once, Tony didn't correct him.

Their chauffeur-driven BMW rolled through the countryside, transporting the three of them to the film studio. Through the tinted windows, the trees slowly became buildings and the birds became people. The people went about their business. They were heading to the local shops, walking with their friends, just hanging out on street corners, ready for the day ahead.

It was all so ordinary.

Ordinary.

When Zak had been ordinary his every waking moment was focused on becoming different. He didn't want to be like everyone else. He wanted to be a star, a somebody.

Now he was no longer ordinary. His new life wasn't ordinary. Nobody else had achieved what Zak had. And yet, as he watched the ordinary people going about their ordinary lives, he couldn't help but feel jealous.

Why couldn't he be like them? They could do anything they wanted…

Zak closed his eyes and imagined what his Redwood Rovers teammates were doing. He imagined that the car he was in was heading for the cup final. He imagined pulling on his cherished number 10 shirt. He imagined cutting through the field and squaring the ball to Chloe for her to score the winning goal – just like he should have done at the start of all this mess. Why hadn't he squared that pass? Why had he played up to the camera so much? No, this wasn't the time to feel guilty. He couldn't feel guilty. For now, he had a job to do.

'Showtime!' Tony shouted from the front seat. They'd arrived. *Pine Green Film Studios, quality in motion since 1987*, a towering sign above the entrance announced. Despite its age, the building looked like one of the warehouses Zak had learned about in his Industrial Revolution classes. The outside was whitewashed yet faded, greyed by the test of time. Hundreds of dull windows stared back at him, each one spaced a metre apart. White curtains were drawn in half of them. A huge air conditioning unit whirred on top of the building, an almost perfectly rectangular box. It felt a million miles from the glitz and glamour of Hollywood. Zak followed his agent through the front door of the studio and found himself in an open plan reception room. At least that was more welcoming. He settled into a deep leather sofa and watched the bustle of workers going about their tasks, racing down corridors with scripts in their hands, chasing after rogue camera assistants. A chance to relax. For a second. Before Zak had even switched off slightly, he was up again, ordered along to film studio number three. Obediently he followed the group down the long corridors, the sound of his footsteps echoing around the walls. He wanted the shoot to be over already. If only he could just be in and out in record time. If only.

The harsh glare of artificial light streamed into a singular spot in the industrial film studio, illuminating the dust that swirled up toward the metal framework of the roof. The room had been made up like the bathroom in a modern house, ready for the filming to take place. Everything was white. The toilet, the sink, the floor. Even the bath mat. The rest of the room was dark, manned by tens of camera crew and assistants and producers, all of them in black t-shirts and jeans. Baller B sat in a corner, wearing his B merchandise. A familiar face. A 'friend'. The pair nodded at each other in mutual respect. Both would be part of the filming process. Upon seeing Tony, the director lit up herself and gave him a familiar hug. After all, it had been Tony who had supplied both him and Baller B for the shoot.

'Hey, TekkerZak!' a young black t-shirted assistant with a cheeky grin nudged him. He barely appeared old enough to be working in a film studio. 'Welcome, man. Can I have a selfie before we get going?'

One selfie led to two, then three, then four. People came up to him and told him they loved his content. Snap out of it, Zak told himself as he posed for yet another selfie. This is what you've always wanted. This is the attention you craved.

And just for that moment, Zak managed to convince himself that his new life was pretty great.

YouTube subscribers: 1,354,296
Instagram followers: 953,094
Twitter followers: 191,623

'Cut!'

The director's voice bellowed across the studio, followed immediately by the harsh sound of the clapperboard. As one, the camera crew stopped filming yet again. 'Sorry, Zak, sorry, but it's not right,' she said as she strode across the studio. 'We're called Perfect Whites because everything has to be perfect. Now, the last 32 takes were great, but they weren't perfect. Your timing at the end was just slightly off. After balancing the ball, we need you to look at the camera straight away. So can we go from the top?'

Zak's energy was fast running out. After being introduced to all of the film crew, he had been taken through hair and make-up so he was ready to face the studio lights. That was four hours ago. He was still at it, doing the same routine over and over.

There was nothing fast about filming. After every take it took at least five minutes to get everything back into the same position. It was a long, dull day of routine.

All Zak wanted was for it to be over.

He was so tired. All he wanted was to sleep. But he couldn't. Because he had to film for Perfect Whites, and then he had to film his own content. Could he fake illness? Pretend that he was sick? Maybe. But then he'd have to start all over again and come back on another day. He couldn't afford to take another whole day to shoot a toothpaste advert. He'd just have to grin and bear it.

If he was going to become the biggest YouTuber on the planet, he'd have to do what he was told.

There was no time to be tired.

The routine started again. As actors embraced and as teeth danced around him, Zak flicked up a white ball and caught it on his head. He rolled the ball down his face and kissed it, then returned it to his forehead. Just like he'd done in so many of his videos before. With the ball perfectly balanced, he reached for his toothbrush and started to brush his teeth. From there, he manoeuvred the ball onto the tip of the toothbrush and balanced it there.

'Perfect Whites – for smiles that are famous,' Zak winked into the camera.

'Cut!'

The director's voice rang loud once again. 'Good, Zak. Good. I just think you can perfect it even more. I'd like to see you do exactly what you just did, but raise the toothbrush another twenty centimetres higher.'

When was it going to end?

With everyone back in their positions, Zak went through his routine once more. Only this time was different. When he went to flick the ball up onto his head he mistimed the movement and the ball cannoned off into one of the cameras.

'Cut! Come on, Zak. Back to starting positions everyone.'

After five minutes of reshuffling, they were ready for the 35th take. Zak's eyelids felt heavy. With all of his effort he forced himself to keep them from shutting. Just one more time, he told himself. Once more and it'll be over. Again, Zak flicked up the ball, and again he mistimed the movement. The ball flicked over Zak's head and dribbled away.

'Cut!'

Zak screamed out in anger at dropping the ball. He was almost done. And then he heard the sniggering. From his position behind the cameras, Baller B was laughing at him. Blood rushed to Zak's face, his cheeks turning a bright shade of pink. He was embarrassed, but he was also angry. How could Baller B mock him when he couldn't do half of the things that Zak could? Zak could see Baller B's phone poking out from between two of the camera crew. He was recording everything. Probably having a laugh with all of his followers at Zak's expense. Well, Zak would show him.

Zak returned to his position, his tiredness suddenly forgotten. He was ready to put on the greatest show Perfect Whites had ever seen. If it was good enough at Brown's Sporting Goods, good enough at the Camp Nou, then he knew his performance could be good enough for a tube of toothpaste.

Zak focused on the ball, took three deep breaths and muttered to himself.

Showtime.

With the dancing teeth actors in place, Zak flicked up the ball and caught it on his forehead. The ball stopped dead still, as if it was glued to Zak's head. One, two, three. The timing was perfect. Zak rolled the ball down his face to give it the kiss. His lips moved in anticipation. And stayed in anticipation. Something had gone wrong. The ball wasn't there. It was bouncing on the floor.

'Cut!'

Zak couldn't believe it. He'd messed up again.

Tony strode toward him. Every step was fuelled with frustration. They were stomps more than anything. 'Come on, Zak,' he hissed, his perfect white teeth glimmering in anger. 'You're better than this.'

The studio was silent. For a matter of seconds, nobody knew what to say. Zak stood panting, his gaze locked on Tony, daring him to say something else. And then it started up again from behind the cameras. Baller B was sniggering once more, his phone pointed straight at Zak's failure.

Zak saw red.

He hated this. He hated everything about his new life and his new friends and his *enabler*. He hated his lack of freedom and the way he was used. He hated his every movement being filmed. He hated having to sacrifice everything he had once loved. He missed his old life. Playing *FIFA* with Chloe. Laughing at Marcus's cut knees. Latching on to Josh's long-range passes. Rolling his eyes at Chris's exaggerations. Even school. The normality of the bell ringing and pupils just like him spilling out onto the playground. This wasn't normal. This had never been what he had wanted. He'd given up everything that he wanted to chase something that he thought he wanted. And this was his reward.

'No, Tony. I'm not!' he shouted at his agent. 'I've already done this stupid advert. What's the point of doing it again and again? I've already given my best. I'm too tired to do anything else. You've been pushing me and pushing me and now I want it to stop. I'm done!'

Words came out of Zak's mouth but he had no control over them. His legs moved without him realising. He took aim and fired, launching the ball toward the cameras. The crew dived out of the way. There was only one person who didn't see it coming. The ball crashed into Baller B's phone and forced it from his hands, then carried on in its pathway, smashing into his shocked face. Zak didn't stay to watch Baller B take several steps back in surprise. He didn't stay to watch the phone fall to the floor. Before he knew it, he'd turned his back on Tony and stormed off the film set.

'Erm, let's take five minutes everyone?' the director suggested as Zak's dad chased after him.

'Wait!' he called. 'Zak!'

But Zak kept on walking. Nobody could stop him now.

Zak was going to walk out of that door and never come back. Until an idea popped into his head.

The perfect idea to create a new perfect life.

YouTube subscribers: 1,356,049
Instagram followers: 953,620
Twitter followers: 191,701

'Come on, son. I know it's exhausting but you're on the final push now.' His dad had caught up with him and had his arms wrapped around him. 'There'll be no pressure on you. Just do what you can and shoot it to the best of your ability. You don't want to let all of these people down, do you?'

Zak let his dad speak to him, allowed himself to be dragged back toward the studio. Zak assured his dad that he had calmed down, then went over to Tony to apologise.

'I should think so,' Tony replied. He then leaned in close, so close that only Zak could hear him. 'Don't forget that I made you the star you are today. Without me you're nothing.'

Zak smiled his biggest, fakest smile. Tony hadn't made him a star. He'd made himself a star. It was him who had performed all of those skills, not Tony. Him who had starred in all of those videos, not Tony. 'Yes, Mr Curtis. Thank you, Mr Curtis. Just give me two minutes.'

Ducking out of the studio quickly, Zak followed the corridor round to the bathroom. It was empty and he shut himself inside one of the plain cubicles. Safely hidden, he checked in his backpack for the faded tube that he had held onto ever since his hamstring strain. His insides danced as his hand latched on to it. He unscrewed the top and squeezed. Zak smiled as the clear liquid touched his skin. There was more than enough.

Showtime.

The film studio was once again a hive of activity. With Zak back on the scene everyone needed to be rushed back to their starting places. 'Sorry again, Mr Curtis.' Tony could barely even look at him.

'Fine,' he replied.

'This Perfect Whites stuff is actually pretty good,' Zak carried on cheerily. 'Look at this. You just put it on your teeth and gums and it cleans them better than normal brushing does. It saves so much time!'

That interested Tony. His teeth glimmered as he looked down at the plain tube Zak had in his hands.

'It's a sample they gave me,' Zak explained. 'Want to try?'

If there was one thing that Tony couldn't resist, it was perfect teeth.

He took the tube from Zak's grasp and squeezed a generous portion onto his fingers. Turning away from Zak once again, he rubbed the liquid onto his teeth and gums.

And then he screamed.

He screamed and screamed and couldn't stop.

'What is it?' Zak's dad rushed straight to Tony. 'Mr Curtis, what's up?'

'It burns!' Tony screamed. 'It burns!'

'What burns?'

'This liquid. It burns so much!'

Zak's dad looked down to the floor where the empty tube had been thrown by Tony. He recognised it. It wasn't a whitening product. It wasn't even a Perfect Whites product. It was the Deep Heat.

'Zak!' he called out. 'Zak!' He spun round and round, searching frantically. But Zak was nowhere to be seen.

In panic, his dad ran to the exit, all the time scanning the area for a sign of Zak. Nothing. He flung open the door and gasped.

Zak's phone was on the concrete pavement outside. He could recognise the distinctive case anywhere. That was to one side. Immediately next to the case was Zak's phone.

Or what was left of Zak's phone.

Shards littered the pavement. Specks of glass were everywhere.

The phone was no more.

Zak wasn't coming back.

It was over.

YouTube subscribers: 1,356,293
Instagram followers: 953,704
Twitter followers: 191,710

The plan worked to perfection. In the commotion, Zak had been able to slip out of the fire exit from the film studios unnoticed.

His heart pounded as he sprinted away from his new life. As the outside world descended on him in its beaming sunlight and chirping birds, Zak felt truly free. He'd done something for himself. Not because Tony had told him to. Not because his followers had wanted him to. It felt so good, to feel free. The phone in his pocket suddenly felt too bulky, its weight playing on his mind. He paused to grab hold of it one last time. He turned it in his hand, thinking back to all of the times he had been unable to put it down. That small piece of aluminium had given him this life. On that phone he'd gained the followers who had given him so many amazing opportunities. It had been the making of him. It had been his prison.

Zak removed the phone from its case and raised it high into the air, then threw it with all of his force. The black aluminium bounced off the pavement once, twice, then came to a rest. Glass shattered over the tarmac until it had broken into hundreds of tiny fragments. The weight in his pocket had been lifted. His prison had been destroyed.

Finally, he was disconnected.

He was no longer @therealTekkerZak. Finally, he could be the real Zak.

He ran forward and turned a sharp left out of the car park and then cut across a grassy verge and through an estate.

He was disconnected but he could still be caught. The fear of being chased was constant. Zak looked round constantly, expecting to see his dad or Tony or the director in hot pursuit.

Sweat pooled underneath his wristwatch. He flicked his wrist up and checked the watch, a present from Tony for getting to 500,000 followers.

14:16. On set Zak had been so tired. Now, he felt more energised than ever before.

14:16. The match! They must have kicked off by now. Zak was sure that the game was supposed to start at 2pm.

There was only one way to find out.

Zak knew that all cup finals took place at the City Rangers stadium. That couldn't be more than a few miles from where he was. He could just head to the main road and follow the signs. Already, he could hear traffic roaring in the distance. He knew the general direction he needed to head in. If only he'd brought his bike! With no money in his pocket, Zak's only option was to run it.

He had his Panther Sports Grantito trainers on. They'd be fine to run in. He could also play in them. Someone could lend him shinpads. The kit would be there.

Cars sped past him as he ran on the verge of the main road. They beeped their horns as he weaved in and out of the trees and bushes, occasionally stepping foot into the road.

Every minute, he looked at the watch on his wrist.

14:24. He could see the city up ahead. Closer now, but still plenty of distance to go. Had there been a goal yet?

Every step felt so good. Being disconnected felt so good. He was 'analogue.' That's what all of the social media stars called it. Analogue, using old-fashioned road signs and an old-fashioned wristwatch without a phone in sight. Just like in the old days.

14:26. Zak's feet pounded the pavement. He'd always been a natural runner. PE teacher after PE teacher had asked him to take long-distance running more seriously. He had been his school's best runner, but football had always been his first love. How could he have run more when every moment had been dedicated to football?

14:28. Zak didn't know how his teammates would react. He hadn't seen or spoken to any of them for so long. Would they even let him play with them?

14:32. Another sign. A brown road sign indicating that the City Rangers stadium was one mile away. More than halfway there. Sweat was pouring down his face. Not long now. All of the pent-up anger and aggression from being told what to do every waking hour was driving him on, forcing his legs forwards.

14:37. Zak hadn't run this distance for a long time. He'd barely run any distance since turning his back on Redwood Rovers. Or rather, since he'd had his back turned.

14:40. The half-time whistle must be close. Still plenty of time left. It only took a second to score a goal. Maybe Redwood wouldn't need to score any more goals. Perhaps they were fine without him.

Perhaps Zak didn't mind.

It wasn't so much about the match, Zak realised, but about being with his old mates. With Redwood he'd always been free to do as he pleased. As he ran past a supermarket, then the local church, he saw them. Four floodlights reaching high into the pale blue sky.

Zak was close.

Still he checked his tracks, looking left, right and behind for his pursuers.

Nothing.

Closer now. Even closer. And then he was there, the City Rangers stadium appearing before him. The entrance gates were open. Zak headed straight through. On the other side, the lush green pitch sat waiting.

Friends and family members littered the side of the pitch. They were slouched over the advertising boards and chatting quietly in the stands. They were holding posters of support and laughing in happiness. From the press box, Cynthia Johnson scribbled as furiously as ever.

The pitch was empty. Zak checked his watch again. 14:48. It must have been half-time.

'Hey up, Zak!' Mr Smith shouted incredulously from the

stands. Zak turned, his face already red from the sheer effort of getting to the game. The usually mild-mannered man looked as if he'd seen a ghost. He raised himself up from his seat in the stands and stared and stared. 'What the blooming hell are you doing here?'

'Hi, Mr Smith. Hi, Mrs Smith,' he panted. 'Chloe told me you needed a striker.'

'I think you owe her an apology first,' Mrs Smith replied curtly. She looked at Zak with suspicion, a far cry from the friendly welcomes of a lifetime.

'I do,' Zak admitted. 'I've been a terrible mate.' What's more, he truly meant it. He felt terrible.

'Well get down there then,' Mrs Smith replied. 'Say your apologies and then get your kit on. There's a game to be won. We're losing 1-0.' Chloe's mother, usually so calm, jabbed her finger in the direction of the tunnel.

'Thanks, Mr and Mrs Smith,' Zak said in relief before racing down the tunnel and following the sign for the changing room.

Already he could hear Mr Jones's voice. It was muffled at first, but as Zak got closer to the door it became clearer. He could picture them all inside, his former teammates. He could see his cherished number 10 shirt still hanging from its peg. He could picture its faint creases, smell its familiar dampness, touch its proud badge.

He stopped himself at the door and took three deep breaths. Steadying himself, he focused on the door and put his fingers to the handle. With his free hand he wiped his sweaty brow, then shook out his stiffening limbs.

'Showtime,' he whispered.

YouTube subscribers: 1,356,301
Instagram followers: 953,711
Twitter followers: 191,712

'What the hell are you doing here?' Mr Jones stared in bewilderment at the just-opened door, his tactics talk momentarily forgotten. All around him his teammates stared too, totally stunned.

It wasn't quite the reaction Zak had expected.

What could he say? Should he apologise and beg to be subbed on? He didn't know, and so as casually as he could, Zak raised his hand. 'Hi, everyone.'

Still, silence. Zak took a step toward the bench, then another one. Nobody stopped him. 'I... I heard you were short of a player,' he said quietly.

Eventually it was Mr Jones who spoke. 'We were. That's why

we brought Gareth in. My rules are still the same: if you don't train then you don't play.'

'But Mr Jones! We're losing. We need Zak!' Chris protested. It had been a long time since one of his friends had stood up for him. Silently Zak thanked him.

'Come on. There's no chance of Gareth scoring for us!' Marcus added. Gareth, sitting next to him, nodded in agreement. Mr Jones looked around at his players, all of them nodding along and sighed. He was a natural born leader. He read books and listened to podcasts on leadership. He preached discipline and prepared to the very best of his ability. But he also valued trust highly. By listening to his players, he would build their trust. Maybe that was just what they needed in the situation.

'Are you sure that this is where you want to be right now?' Mr Jones asked, his voice firm yet fair.

'Totally.' He replied truthfully.

Mr Jones's next movements were short, sharp and measured. He wheeled round from Zak to his son. 'Right, Gareth. Off you get,' he announced. 'Good effort, kiddo. Great discipline in fighting for us.'

'Thank goodness,' a haggard-looking Gareth replied. 'I don't think I could have survived another half.'

'Here you go, Zak,' Mr Jones rummaged round the kit bag and pulled out a match shirt. 'It's not your normal number but it'll have to do.' Zak caught it and turned the shirt round. Number 12. That was fine. Anything to get back onto that pitch.

He took off his sweat-drenched Panther Sports t-shirt and once again wore the navy blue of Redwood Rovers. From his left-hand side, someone knocked Zak's arm. It was Gareth.

'Need these?' he asked, holding a pair of shin pads. 'I wore them for the first time today. They're a bit sweaty. but they'll do the job.'

Gratefully, Zak took the shin pads from Gareth, making sure to wipe them on his shirt before placing them on his bare legs. The stench made his insides turn but they'd have to do.

'So, where were we?' Mr Jones asked. 'Yes, that's it. Discipline. We need to be more disciplined. Stay in our 4-4-2 formation. Lizzie, Chris, I don't want you drifting. Stay in your shape. Sometimes we're getting overrun in midfield. That's where they got their goal. When we can, get the ball to Chloe. Chloe, you're playing an absolute blinder. Keep going and your goal will come.'

Chloe nodded at Mr Jones. She was in the zone. Her eyes were focused directly at Mr Jones, listening to his every word. Even Zak's presence hadn't yet distracted her. Nor did that surprise Zak. Why should she pay him any attention after the way he had treated her?

'Zak,' Mr Jones added. 'I need you to support Chloe. Come short so she can run long behind the defence. Try and pass to her when you can.' Zak nodded at Mr Jones. He wasn't in a position to do anything else.

'Right, I think that's it,' Mr Jones finished. 'Anything else from anyone?'

Chloe stood up and pulled her captain's armband tight around her bicep. 'What are we waiting for? Let's do it!'

Several players cheered as they got up from the bench.

'This game is ours to win!' Chloe declared to the team. She moved toward the door, high fiving each and every player to gee them up. Just like Zak used to do, he realised. With all of the players now out of the changing room he motioned to run after them but found an arm blocking his path. Chloe. 'You've got a lot of making up to do, you know,' she hissed. 'You best start now.'

With that she was gone out of the door. Zak never even had a chance to reply.

YouTube subscribers: 1,356,312
Instagram followers: 953,718
Twitter followers: 191,714

Football is a simple game made complicated by people who should know better. Or so the saying goes. In reality, Zak found, football was a simple game made much more complicated by lack of practice. Fatigue from his breathless race to the game wasn't helping, either.

Chloe had been right. Zak's skills looked cool in videos. They were sick. But they weren't actually that useful. In a full-blooded match, it turned out, defenders didn't just sit back and applaud as he flicked the ball from body part to body part. They didn't like, share and subscribe as a result. Instead, they charged. Zak's attempted flicks and tricks were like a red flag to a bull. And the bull kept on winning.

Within a minute, Zak had been flattened.

Within two minutes, Zak had been flattened again.

His teammates gave him little sympathy. 'Come on, Zak,' Mr Jones roared from the side. 'Move the ball. Pass. Move. Pass. Move. Don't let the defenders have the chance to get close to you.'

Zak tried to manipulate the ball as he always had. He tried to pass the ball at pace and make dynamic runs. Yet everything he did was much slower than he remembered. The match was being played at breakneck speed. Surely games didn't used to be this fast? How had Zak ever coped, let alone flourished?

Focus. You can do this. You are good enough. You have the ability. Zak repeated the words over and over again in his head. *Showtime. Showtime. Showtime.*

Whenever he had struggled in the past, Mr Jones always encouraged him to get back to the basics. When you make an easy pass, your confidence grows, Mr Jones said. If you keep on making easy passes then you'll get enough confidence to make a hard pass.

For the next ten minutes, that's what Zak focused on. He could control the controllables. A five-yard pass backwards to Chris. A first-time lay-off to Chloe. A header won against the opposing defender.

Slowly, his legs seemed to gain more energy. Despite the demands of the day, Zak's limbs ached less. Confidence was beginning to flow through his body.

Slowly, Redwood were starting to control the game. They were having most of the possession. Chloe clanged a shot off the post, then a long-range effort from Lizzie just skimmed the crossbar. The crowd gasped, then applauded. They were dotted around the stadium, their noise reverberating around the Teflon roof and driving the players on. For once, they weren't all staring at him. Zak was just one of the twenty-two players on the pitch. There was nothing special about him.

Redwood's opponents, Riverside, were doing everything they could to keep the ball out of their net. Under the increasing pressure, their defence became even more narrow, squeezing even more space away from Redwood.

The game was now all being played in Riverside's half. Chloe was running the show, creating chances from nothing and making their defenders look silly. But Riverside's players were defending as if their lives depended on it, making last-ditch tackles and goal-saving clearances to thwart Chloe and her teammates.

'How long, ref?' Riverside's captain, a diminutive midfielder with bundles of energy, asked. The referee checked her watch and signalled that there were five minutes of normal time remaining.

More than enough. It only takes a second to score a goal.

Riverside had all eleven players defending deep in their own half. Redwood would get past two, three, four players with their pass and move football. But there were always more defenders in the way.

Shots were attempted from long range but easily gathered by the Riverside keeper.

Redwood were becoming desperate. Normal time was up. They just had whatever the referee added for stoppage time left to get an equaliser.

Redwood made several passes on the right wing and then switched the ball quickly. Riverside weren't prepared. Their defence was too far over to where the ball had been. Zak, who had been trying to find space on the edge of the 18-yard area, suddenly found himself free. Charging forward from his centre back position, Josh spotted the opportunity and sent a pass slicing through Riverside's defence, and all of a sudden Zak was through on goal.

He couldn't believe his luck.

The ball bounced lovingly into the instep of his Panther Sports Grantito trainers and then nestled just in front of him. Now, all he focused on was the net. The Riverside keeper rushed out to narrow the angle. Riverside's defenders charged back to try and prevent Zak's shot. Zak had been in this position hundreds of times. He judged where the keeper was coming from, how fast he was travelling, and the area of the goal left open. He thought of his redemption, of how scoring would help him be forgiven. And then, out of the corner of his eye, he saw Chloe. She had run into the box and lost her marker. She was free. In front of her, the goal was gaping.

Zak shaped to shoot, just as he had done so many times in the past. He brought his foot forward and then adjusted it at the last moment so that the ball went square instead. The keeper hadn't expected it, Riverside's defenders hadn't expected it, but Chloe had.

The only problem was that Chloe had expected the ball to be played to her feet. Zak's pass wasn't clean, the ball coming more off the toe than the instep. As Chloe moved forward for a certain goal, the ball moved backwards. Desperately, she attempted to adjust her body, twisting around with all of her effort. It wasn't enough. The ball rolled centimetres behind her. It should have been an easy pass. It should have been an easy goal. But instead, it was nothing. Riverside cleared the ball to safety and cheered with relief.

There wasn't even enough time left for Redwood to take the throw-in. The referee put the whistle to her lips and blew three short, sharp times.

Game over.

Zak collapsed to the floor. He couldn't believe it. The energy drained from him. How could his pass have been so bad? He'd ruined it for everyone. They'd lost and it was all his fault. First the film studio, now this. Zak wished that the ground would open and swallow him whole. He banged his head against the ground, closing his eyes and replaying the pass over and over in his head.

He'd never felt worse.

From above him he could hear the cheers of Riverside's players and the warm applause of the crowd. He could sense footsteps running to meet and celebrate together. Yet all he could see was the darkness of the earth. He lay there, face down, for what felt like minutes.

A hand on his shoulder. Zak ignored it. He couldn't bear to face anyone. Another hand, this time on his other shoulder. It was shaking him. Zak opened his eyes and turned to see his best mate standing above him.

'Well played, Zak,' Chloe said softly. 'You tried to do the right thing. That means more than the result.' With the help of Mr Jones, she lifted him to his feet.

'You showed great discipline, Zak,' Mr Jones added. 'You've made me proud. You've all made me proud.'

A pair of arms were placed around Zak. It was Chloe. She was hugging him. Zak's body remained limp. He couldn't bring himself to hug her back. He didn't deserve her. Chloe let go, only for Chris to hug him. Why were they doing this? He'd disappeared, then ruined everything for them. Raising his head from Chris's soiled shirt, he saw his other teammates slowly approaching. A mixture of desperate disappointment and brave faces, yet none of them angry at him. None of them telling him he was useless or better than that.

For a mad second, Zak felt like crying. Really crying. He felt like bawling his eyes out and ridding himself of all that had happened in the last few months.

How could he have been so stupid?

Why had he allowed himself to become so obsessed with followers?

Followers didn't matter. Across his social media channels he had well over a million. Yet none of them had helped him at the film studio. None of them had given him the freedom to play football. They hadn't supported him in his time of need. Neither had his new friends, the powerful YouTubers. They'd only laughed at him. And what good had his agent done? He had overworked Zak, used him, put pressure on him and taken away all of his freedom.

From the space between his teammates, Zak could catch glimpses of the crowd. There was Cynthia Johnson, still scribbling furiously. There were Mr and Mrs Smith, clapping graciously. The familiarity of it all was just so reassuring, so satisfying. There were others that Zak recognised, parents and friends of his old mates. There was – wait, no. Zak did a double take. And again. Surely not? He blinked but nothing changed. The man was still there. He was clapping and clapping. Zak looked even closer and saw the man wiping a tear from his eye. The man made eye contact with Zak and waved.

Zak waved back. He couldn't help but smile.

It was his dad.

And there wasn't a video camera in sight.

YouTube subscribers: 3,130,222
Instagram followers: 1,601,745
Twitter followers: 386,203

HEARTBREAK FOR REDWOOD
By Cynthia Johnson

Promising local football side Redwood Rovers had their cup final dreams dashed by Riverside.

With injuries and suspensions causing havoc with Redwood's team, coach Adam Jones recalled former star striker turned superstar YouTuber Zak Oxden for a cameo appearance in the second half.

But it was to no avail, as Jones's players fell to a 1-0 defeat. Despite captain Chloe Smith's heroics, Redwood were unable to conjure an equaliser. Smith twice hit the post and Lizzie Durden skimmed the bar, while Oxden squandered a golden opportunity with the last kick of the game.

'I'm proud of my players,' said Jones. 'They fought with one of the best teams in the county and dominated the game at times. They will have learned a lot about themselves and I'm excited for the next stage of their development.'

'I'm obviously gutted but it's a privilege to share the pitch with these players,' captain Smith added. 'There's an unbelievable team spirit and we have a special bond. Nothing can break it – not even a defeat such as the one we've suffered.'

With no fixtures remaining, Redwood will now set their sights on league and cup success next season, where they will once again be competing at the highest level. If you're interested in playing for Redwood, please contact Adam Jones on info@redwoodrovers.com for a trial.

'About time we got some trialists in. I could do with a new strike partner.' Chloe scrunched the paper up and threw it at Zak. 'One that could square a pass instead of flicking it up and catching it on their forehead.'

'Shut up. You only started playing well when I left. I had to stop playing so you could come out from my shadow,' Zak replied, trying and failing to hide his laughter.

'Yeah, I'm just like your YouTube channel,' Chloe said. 'When you left I got better, and when you stopped posting videos on YouTube, your channel has got better. Nobody has to see your rubbish videos anymore and you've got even more followers because of it.'

Chloe had a point. It had been weeks since he had posted

a video and yet his following had increased more than ever. He had Baller B to thank for that. Baller B's sneaky filming of Zak's anger had been all over the internet. 'FREESTYLER MELTDOWN!!!' screamed the video. Baller B had even used a cover photo of Zak screaming at Tony, his face red with anger.

It couldn't have been more embarrassing.

Yet people had loved it. Reaction videos were all over the internet. Followers flocked to his page. Viewers became fans.

Not that it mattered to Zak. He barely checked his social media anymore. He'd bought a new phone which had no internet access. It was a brick. One that boasted about having polyphonic ringtones. All Zak needed it for was speaking to his mates. If he wanted to go on the internet he could go on a computer.

He wasn't going to get rid of his social media. His dad suggested it might be for the best, but Zak was still proud of what he'd done. He'd worked hard to build his following and felt there was no need for it to go to waste. In time he might even film more videos. What he couldn't do, however, was get carried away.

Everything was about balance.

Everything was about priority. His friends were his priority. His family was his priority. Once again, football was a priority. Social media was not.

'Hello! Is anyone there?' Chloe woke Zak from his deep thoughts.

'You what?' he asked.

'I mean, I know you're bad at *FIFA* but I've just walked through your defence. I've mugged you right off. And it's 5-0 now so you best score quick or you owe me a written apology.'

'You play nice now, Chloe.' Mrs Smith was looking in from the doorway.

'Hey up, Zak, just been with your dad,' Mr Smith added from behind her. 'Good to see him doing well for himself. I always knew he would end up helping others.'

'He's smashing it, Mr Smith,' Zak said, his cheeks burning. 'I'm buzzing for him.'

'Well we are too,' Mrs Smith added. 'We worried about him after the factory went—' Mr Smith nudged her in the ribs before she could finish her sentence. Zak knew what she was going to say, though.

'Don't worry, Mrs Smith,' Zak said, taking it in his stride. 'Having no work hit Dad hard. That's why he put so much effort into my videos. He wanted to escape and forget all about it. Now he's learned a lot and he's putting that same effort in, but for other people. He's doing really well with it.'

'That's great,' Mr and Mrs Smith said in unison.

They closed the door and left Chloe and Zak alone once more. Time had helped their friendship return. Zak's new life was in the past. His old life was in the present.

Freestyling with Ronaldinho had been incredible, but it didn't come close to the pleasures of a kickabout in Chloe's back garden.

Walking out at the Camp Nou was unreal, but not a patch on Redwood Rovers' park pitch.

Launching his own merchandise on national TV was sick, but not as sick as an epic best-of-five on *FIFA* with Chloe.

And pretty much anything was better than filming a toothpaste advert.

This was his new old life. It was sick. It was everything that he had ever wanted.

And he no longer needed Tony to tell him otherwise.

POLARIS

PUBLISHING